BILLY MAKIN

JIHADA 2
A BRIDE FOR ALLAH

Published by B and M Publishers UK

ISBN: 978-0-9955533-5-4 (Print)
ISBN: 978-0-9955533-4-7 (Mobi)

CONTENTS

INTRODUCTION

FATHER CHRISTMAS

In days of old, when I was a child, I guess about 8 years of age, I watched in horror as my father bricked up our open coal fireplace.

'How is Father Christmas going to come down the chimney at Christmas and deliver my presents?' I asked.

Around the same time, a little 8 year old Muslim girl in a far off country asked her father about Allah.

The next day at my school, the entire class sat in stunned silence as the teacher confirmed my father's words.

FATHER CHRISTMAS DOES NOT EXIST

Perhaps that was the day when I started to grow into a young adult.

My young mind began to question the world around me.

It began to challenge and cast doubts on the things that I had previously taken for granted.

It kick started the process that had been instrumental in leading the Western World into becoming the most advanced and free society the human race has ever known.

The little girl was stoned to death and her father beheaded. The Iman at the local Mosque wasn't too happy with either the question or the answer.

Fourteen hundred years of Islamic progress had regressed fourteen hundred years by that one act.

Now.

I am sad to report that our Western Civilization
is about to follow.

There is no way back.

We have already lost.

CHAPTER 1

IN DREAMS

Susan Clarke awoke from her brief dream with a start.

The sharp stabbing pain between her legs was not part of the dream.

She had been dreaming of home – a warm loving home in a cold and wet country.

Cold and wet sounded like heaven.

She wanted to be cold and wet – she could barely remember what it was like to be cold and wet.

She especially wanted to be wet.

She wanted to feel the soothing warm water engulf her; cleansing, sanitizing, and washing away the memories of countless men – dirty stinking men – violent sadistic men – men with no morals, no scruples, and no semblance of the supposed compassion that separates the human race from the animals that these men had now become.

There was an over bearing gagging smell of sweat in the darkened room. It lingered with unseen malice around the fringes of rancid rotting fish – maybe meat; an obnoxious cocktail sprinkled with tobacco – possibly a hint of rum or whiskey, competing against a background laden with vomit.

The air was hot and sticky, and seemed to contain barely enough oxygen to breath properly.

She wanted to be sick.

There had been no rotting fish, no sweat, tobacco, rum or whiskey in her dream – just a warm loving home in a cold and wet country.

She wanted to close her legs and squeeze them tightly together; so tight that no man would ever again be able to enter – to use – to abuse, ever, ever again.

How many more of them would there be today?

Was this number 6 or maybe number 7?

It no longer mattered. Numbers were unimportant. The pain and the shame were important – the numbers were irrelevant, she had long ago stopped counting. Yesterday she had taken 7 men. Seven stinking, sweaty, bearded, sadistic bastards, and all for the supposed love of Allah.

'Fuck Allah.' Her lips mouthed the words, but no sound came out.

She was no more than a plaything to them – a worthless toy – something for them to stick their dicks in – a sperm receptacle – sub human. Not even animals were treated with such disrespect – such contempt.

Susan thought of the many ways that she could now describe herself and realized that she was all of these, but she had to find a place for her mind that was being neither abused nor buggered.

She tried to take her mind home.

Home was Leeds in England.

It stubbornly refused to move from its captivity, and remained firmly under the control of her physical presence – venturing out only in dreams.

She could no longer visualize her family, her home, her friends. There was only one mental portal into Leeds, and at the end of that portal was Amir.

Amir was blocking the portal, and there was no way past him.

When the time was right she would go over him – through him – she would destroy him.

The thought sustained Susan.

Her vengeful subconscious helped her physical presence and her mind to remain companions, tenuously bound together when both of them wanted to simply disappear into oblivion – into a nothingness. To disappear into an abstract void where there would be no more pain – no more shame.

Back home in Leeds this had never been the plan.

This was most certainly not why she was now in the Middle East. The Jihadists needed children, brain washed children who would one day fight for the love of Allah.

She was to be "A Bride for Allah", but how many fathers did Allah's first born need?

Amir had never told her about this back home in Leeds.

She closed her eyes and tried to forget the pain that was now accompanying the ever faster rhythmic thrusting and grunting of the overweight, bearded, stinking bastard, who was on the verge of adding to the almost none stop river of semen that had been running between her thighs and onto the dirty bed sheets for the last few weeks.

His breath added to the unique, all-pervading sickening perfume of the room – a perfume that would forever accompany her – a perfume that would overpower all her senses with its own evil malevolence – a perfume concocted in hell.

Amir had never told her about this duty to Allah.

Amir had told her all about the Holy war – the Jihad, and of how his handsome young cousin Mohammad was looking for a bride to bear him good Muslim children.

It had all seemed so simple – so romantic. She would be the wife of a brave and handsome young freedom fighter. She would prepare his meals in the elegant house that Amir had described. She would become a mother to Mohammad's children, and have the respect of all their neighbors as she tended her own little garden – a magical garden filled with exotic and beautifully colored flowers. She would no longer be a school girl taking orders from teachers and parents – she would be a woman and fulfill her obligation to Allah.

She would be "A Bride for Allah".

Where were the flowers she wondered as she tried to blot out the pain?

She closed her eyes even tighter, trying to eliminate the image of the animal jumping up and down on her.

She tried unsuccessfully to picture a pretty English flower garden.

She could see the flowers but not the colors. Why was everything grey – painfully grey – shamefully grey?

The fat Arab on top of her was now grunting like a pig.

He was biting her shoulder. She felt the blood running down her arm and onto the filthy bed sheets.

She tried to smell the grey flowers – they smelled only of sweat – rotting fish – tobacco – whiskey.

There were no gardens here; there weren't even any buildings that were untouched by the never ending war. What flowers could she possibly grow on sand and rock?

Where was Mohammad?

Amir had told her that Mohammad would be waiting for her the moment that she crossed the Turkish border.

Maybe Mohammad was dead.

Maybe Amir had lied.

A thought of dread passed through her head, as for the one hundredth time she considered her predicament. Was this all she had to look forward to now for the rest of her life? Was she to become no more than a human sperm receptacle – an incubating machine for a never ending supply of future Jihadists and suicide bombers?

Fuck Amir – fuck Allah – fuck the man who was now fucking her.

The fat bearded Arab withdrew from her, and with a triumphant shout of "Allahu Akbar", slipped his trousers back on, wiping the blood from his still erect penis with his filthy shirt as he did so.

Susan opened her eyes and saw the blood.

Was she bleeding internally or had her periods started?

'Please be my periods,' she almost said out loud. She no longer wanted to be the mother of any "Bastard Child of Allah". She wanted to go home to Leeds. She wanted to go back to school and finish her exams. She wanted to be an actress. She wanted to see her friends, even her two annoying and tormenting younger brothers. They would be forever forgiven and tolerated, she might even play with them when she had the time.

She wanted to see Amir.

She again closed her eyes, and the Leeds' portal briefly opened to reveal Amir still standing there – grinning.

'Fuck Amir.' This time the words escaped through her clenched teeth. 'Fuck you – fuck you – fuck you.'

A young man climbed on top of her and gently parted her legs, placing one finger over her lips as he did so.

How many more would she have to take today she wondered, and why didn't this one stink like all the others? He smelled almost sweet – a hint of summer roses perhaps? The all-pervading, uniquely sickening stench that never left her prison briefly disappeared, as fond memories of her father's aftershave momentarily invaded her senses.

'I am Mohammad,' he whispered into her ear. 'I am Amir's cousin. There will be no more men today, I have convinced them that the blood on Achmed could be serious. They do not want to lose their most valuable asset; pretty young white girls earn them lots of money. They have agreed for you to come back to my house for a few days. I have gained their trust so we will be safe.'

Both Susan and Mohammad climbed from the bed, Susan suddenly feeling shy and vulnerable. Mohammad was staring at her naked body, and instinctively she grabbed the dirty bed sheet and wrapped it around her, at the same time realizing the stupidity and futility of the gesture. She had never left the room for the last few days, and had been nothing more than a warm, naked sex toy for a countless number of men.

Where had this irrational bout of shyness appeared from?

Could it be the aftershave that had transformed Mohammad into a human being?

The other men she could no-longer see as human – they were no more than animals – they were worse than animals – their actions had relegated them well below the status of any animal in her eyes.

She suddenly remembered her pain.

Her nipples were sore to the touch. They had been squeezed, sucked, bitten, and were now so swollen that to even think of them hurt. They were aggravated by the constant throbbing that came with every heartbeat.

Mohammad saw her pain.

He saw the fresh blood running from her shoulder down onto her breast; he also saw the bruises and the pinch marks that covered almost her entire body. He saw the disgusting brown mixture of semen and blood that was running down her legs.

'We have got to move quickly before they change their minds,' he said. 'Wipe yourself down and clean the blood from your legs, then put this on.'

Mohammad passed her a long black Burka, and after slipping the garment over her head and rearranging it so that her eyes were positioned to see through the slit, Susan made her way slowly and painfully towards the door.

Mohammad held her hand in order to keep her upright; he was aware of the problem.

He had heard the men boasting of how they had ignored Susan's pleas, and delighted in the buggery of such a prized piece of young white Infidel. So what if she had turned Muslim? She was still an Infidel in the eyes of Allah, and any indignity that they chose to inflict on her would certainly meet with Allah's approval.

The two of them left the bullet and shrapnel scarred breeze block building and walked across 30 or so yards of sand, stone, and broken glass.

Susan regretted forgetting her shoes, as a piece of glass pierced her instep. It was too late to turn back, her only hope of salvation from this living hell being the waiting vehicle.

Mohammad helped Susan into his white Toyota pick-up, and walking around the front of the vehicle, climbed in himself.

He turned the ignition key – there was no response.

Susan Clarke shuddered beneath her newly acquired black prison, and she felt the tears begin to run down her face. Were they tears of relief over her imminent escape from this hell, or was all of this simply some gigantic practical joke – no more than an elaborate charade designed to further humiliate her?

It took 4 attempts before the vehicle coughed and eventually fired up, each failed attempt driving Susan into an ever greater panic of fear and desperation. She sighed audibly with relief at the sound of the 3 litre diesel engine bursting into life. Mohammad turned towards Susan and grinned ruefully before driving away, shouting "Allahu Akbar" at a group of men who were either cleaning or lovingly caressing their Kalashnikov rifles.

The men returned the shout, at the same time gesticulating wildly with sexual hand movements.

'Filthy murdering bastards,' Mohammad said. 'You are safe now Susan.'

Susan Clarke heard nothing.

She was fast asleep, and was dreaming of a warm loving home in a cold and wet country.

CHAPTER 2

A FAMILIAR FACE

Sam Stevens was in a hurry to get home; it was Josh, his younger son's 4th birthday, and he simply could not wait to see the look of delight on his son's face as he wheeled in his new bicycle. All of his son's friends had bikes, and living in a quiet Leeds cul de sac, meant that he would be safe from passing vehicles.

The traffic lights ahead were on green as he pushed his foot down a little harder on the accelerator of the empty bus; with a bit of luck, he may even arrive home before his son and would be able to hide the present. Sam smiled at the thought of his son running around the house looking for it.

Travelling along an adjoining road, David White was also in a hurry, he was also in a good mood; today was pay day, and tonight he would be taking his fiancé out for a meal at one of the many Leeds' curry houses. His bus was full of school children, and the constant sound of shouting, screaming, and laughter, sometimes made concentration difficult. He had been doing the same school run for a couple of years now, and had learned how to block out most of the noise.

The lights ahead of him were on red, and as he touched his brakes, on came the amber light, followed almost immediately by the green. David White failed to notice the unusual behavior of the lights, accelerated, and being slightly distracted by a sudden screaming coming from directly behind him, did not see the bus of Sam Stevens directly in front of him.

The two buses collided with an almighty bang and a shattering of glass; the bus full of school children careering across the road and crashing into the side of a parked car, before coming to a grinding halt as it smashed into a petrol station.

The center of Leeds was rocked by a terrific explosion, as the flying sparks ignited the bus's fuel tank and the petrol that was now erupting from a couple of shattered pumps.

Sam Steven's son would not be hunting for his new bicycle that evening – he had been on the bus.

Two young Asian men had been watching events unfold.

They walked away with a satisfied look on each of their faces. One of them was carrying a video camera, and the younger and smaller one, was carrying a small laptop computer.

The traffic lights were now working normally again.

Professor Jeremy Blythe was walking his dog, Fido, along the road when he saw the flash, followed shortly after by the sound of the explosion.

Fido tried to bolt in alarm, the professor holding tightly onto the lead, before gently lifting the small Jack Russell terrier into his arms, and talking calmly to it in a quiet reassuring voice.

Professor Blythe was the archetypal eccentric academic – the mad professor – he fit the profile perfectly. Who else would dream of naming their dog Fido? He was well respected wherever he went, and to his pupils, was affectionately known as Mr. Bean, after the bumbling creation of Rowan Atkinson, the English comedian.

Mr. Bean was indeed a perfect name for the Professor. There were days when he turned up for school in different colored socks, jumpers that were back to front or inside out; days when he sat in the wrong classroom waiting for his pupils to arrive; days when he turned up for school only to find that the rest of the country were on a bank holiday.

Nevertheless, Mr. Bean loved his work. The knowledge that he himself was imparting knowledge to a whole new generation sustained his interest in his job – his vocation.

Across the road, two young men walked swiftly in the opposite direction before turning right down a side road off the main road, and walking on in the direction of the local Mosque.

Professor Blythe put Fido back onto the ground and stared after the two young men as they disappeared from view. The older and taller of the two men had the typical Muslim beard, but the smaller one had turned his head away as he had passed him. Why, the professor had wondered, and why were they walking away from the explosion? Human nature, coupled with a morbid sense of curiosity, dictated that they would be only too interested in seeing what was happening, yet they had shown not the slightest interest; everywhere else, people were now heading toward the accident.

The smaller of the two men looked vaguely familiar. He was still a boy, a little too young to grow a beard, and he had shielded his face away from the Professors gaze; still, one glance was enough, he had definitely seen him before, but where?

Professor Blythe turned around and began walking back home. Fido had had quite enough excitement for one evening.

He did not want Fido having nightmares.

CHAPTER 3

GENIUS

The class was a little more raucous than usual as Professor Blythe entered the classroom at exactly 9am the next morning; there was a tangible air of morbid excitement.

Everyone seemed to know someone who had died in the previous evening's accident. A hush descended almost immediately. Blythe was confused, this had never happened to him before. Why were his pupils suddenly behaving? Most mornings it took a couple of minutes and a succession of jokingly aimed threats before full order was restored.

He looked around suspiciously, his eyes following the gazes of his class, and sure enough, he had once again been jokingly set up. Sitting in the middle of his desk was a Mr. Bean toy that was sporting an almost imbecilic grin.

Blythe fixed the class with a mock glare before bursting into laughter – the class responded in similar fashion. 'Right, you intellectual pygmies.' He raised his voice and tried unsuccessfully to sound serious. 'Instead of computer studies, today we will do advanced calculus.'

A collective groan followed. The class knew that he was joking, yet the moment was too enjoyable to waste.

Professor Blythe was much too good to be a school teacher, even if he did head his own department. His intellect was almost off the scale, and his computer knowledge was unparalleled – well almost.

Sitting at the back of the class and almost hidden from the professor's sight was Saha.

Saha was not an ordinary pupil. Saha was a mathematical and computer genius.

He had first come to Blythe's attention as a twelve year old who had always managed to score 100% in both computer studies and mathematics. As far as Professor Blythe's memory went back, he could not recall Saha scoring less than 100% in any exam. Saha seemed to have unlimited knowledge of every subject that the professor taught.

Saha never spoke in class. Most pupils were usually only too happy to raise their arm to answer difficult questions, Saha never did. He was invisible, and simply blended in with the furniture, yet always managed to answer any question that Blythe directed at him.

His appearance was equally invisible outside the confines of the classroom. Standing a couple of inches below the 5 foot mark, Saha was easily the smallest boy in the class of 15 year olds, and hadn't grown a fraction of an inch over the last 3 years, while the rest of his schoolboy contemporaries had witnessed the mid teen spurt of several inches.

His lack of height, coupled with his slight frame, and the beginning of an elderly man's stoop due to the early stages of spondylitis, made him a frequent target for bullying.

Saha was also mixed race, his father being Pakistani, and his mother, who whilst still a barely pubescent English schoolgirl, had been groomed into prostitution by one of the many Asian gangs operating around the deprived Leeds' council estates.

Saha barely existed – he was almost unseen – invisible, even when in full view – a loner – a loser – a nobody.

Whenever Blythe had marked either Saha's exam or homework papers, his mind always wandered to the film "Good Will Hunting". Saha was like Will Hunting. He was a genius, but appeared neither to realize it nor care. On more than one occasion, Blythe had slipped a couple of 'ringer' questions into the exam papers in order to see just how far Saha's genius went. Saha still got 100%, even though on occasions Blythe himself had to read up on the answers.

Unknown to Blythe, Saha was also a computer hacker, skilled beyond even Blythe's comprehension. His family never paid council tax, electricity, or water bills. They never paid any bills; he simply hacked into the relevant data base, and altered the family bills to "PAID", or simply removed all traces of the families' existence. Banks had initially proved a little more difficult, but now, he could view and manipulate anyone's account without arousing suspicion.

Someday, he would make a multi-million pound killing. For the time being however, money held little relevance.

There was one slight flaw in the otherwise perfect pupil. Saha was homosexual – Saha loved Amir, and would do anything that his fantasy lover asked him to do.

Amir was strictly heterosexual. Both young men were also Muslim, but the religion not only frowned on homosexuality, in many countries it was an almost certain death sentence.

Unlike Saha, Amir was not insignificant. Still in his early twenties, Amir was going places. Slightly above average height, slim, yet well proportioned, he carried around his own personal aura, which when coupled with his obvious good looks, ensured a succession of young women entered the expensively furnished bedroom of his expensive detached house in one of Leeds' more salubrious districts.

Many of these young women were no longer in the country.

Amir had an expensive lifestyle to maintain, and pretty young girls paid the bills.

Amir was aware of Saha's feelings towards him. These feelings would certainly prove useful in the future, and so for now, he would play along with the fantasy.

Saha was much too valuable to the cause.

Amir often felt sad that Saha would not be joining him in Paradise. Allah would never allow homosexuals to enter Paradise. Even if Saha became a martyr, what use would 72 beautiful young virgins be to him?

Maybe there would be 72 beautiful young boys waiting for Saha – wherever Allah chose to send him; for sure, Saha loved Allah with the same heavenly devotion that he reserved for Amir on earth.

Professor Blythe handed the previous day's test papers to Lizzy who was sitting at the front of the class, and asked her to distribute them. The marks were exceptionally good, many being in the high 80's, one of course was 100%.

As he had marked the papers the previous evening before taking Fido for his evening exercise, he had let out a gasp on reaching Saha's paper. He didn't bother going through the whole paper, why would he bother? He already knew the outcome, and was only interested in the answer to the last question, the Omega 7 Paradox.

He had searched long and hard to find a question that few people in the world would be able to understand, let alone answer.

No one on earth had ever been able to solve the greatest mathematical problem ever encountered. This was simply because there was no answer to the Omega 7 Paradox. He himself had been unable to work it out for almost 3 years at Cambridge University. Night after night he had stayed awake studying Professor Rudolf's book, and night after night he had finally dropped off to sleep in a state of mental trauma and physical exhaustion.

Saha had got it correct. Saha had solved one of the last remaining mysteries on earth. Saha had solved an equation that could not be solved.

Was Saha of greater intellect than Rudolf, the Princeton Professor who had been so tantalizingly close, yet had still failed to solve the problem?

Rudolf was up there with Einstein and Newton, and it had taken him half a lifetime, and the complete loss of his sanity, to almost solve the equation. He had got to within plus or minus 2%, but could never bridge the gap that fully solved the equation. Saha had done it in one evening, completely eliminating the 2%.

Surely no one on Earth was so smart, especially not a 15 year old immature kid?

Saha must have read up on the damned thing and copied it out, but where could he have found the answer from if it had never been solved?

There was certainly nothing on the internet. As far as Blythe was aware, the full, yet incomplete equation, and the cognitive process for solving it, was only contained in one book; a book that he himself had studied during his student days at Cambridge. A book that created the all-consuming obsession that had cost him the first and only love of his life.

Lucy Burroughs, the most beautiful girl that he had ever seen, was not prepared to accept the 10% of his mind that he allowed her access to. Professor Rudolf and the Omega 7 Paradox fully occupied the other 90%, and there was a no entry sign blocking her way.

Professor Blythe looked down the room at Saha who was unassumingly writing something down on his test paper. No one in the world had ever solved the Omega 7 Paradox, so the only conclusion there could possibly be was that Saha had solved it by himself, but how?

Was that the young man, or rather the boy, that he had seen the previous evening walking away from the scene of the crash he wondered? He had only caught a glimpse, yet he certainly looked familiar. The slight stoop and the awkward gate were logged somewhere in his mind.

If it was Saha, why did he turn his head away from him? All of his pupils would certainly acknowledge him if they met him in the street, they all knew Fido, and had played with him on the odd occasion when he had brought him along to the school sports day.

Was Saha concealing something? Surely he couldn't have had anything to do with the crash?

Still – the whole thing looked mighty suspicious.

How could the two young men, possessors of presumably healthy inquisitive young minds, walk away from the biggest thing that had happened in Leeds since their FA cup triumph of 1972 under Revie?

Blythe momentarily closed his eyes. Alan Clarke dived forward. The ball bounced off his forehead into the Arsenal net.

CHAPTER 4

TWO CHOICES

Susan Clarke awoke from what had been a long troubled sleep. She had been dreaming of home, she had also been dreaming of Amir, the same Amir who had promised her the undying love of Allah if she were to secretly convert to Islam and join the Jihadist in the Middle East.

'Why not?' she had said out loud, as Amir had gently made love to her in the comfort of his own home. It was to be an adventure, a break from the boring repetitive life that she was now leading. She was only 15 years old, and if Mohammad, Amir's cousin, was half as handsome and half as wealthy as Amir had described him to be, she may well marry him and happily settle down in a nice warm country, far away from the dreadful Leeds weather.

One day she was going to be a world famous actress, the experience would be invaluable to her career. 'Do they have a film industry in the Middle East?' she had asked Amir.

'Growing, and sure to make a world impact in the near future,' he had told her. 'British actresses were in big demand throughout the Middle East.'

From there, she would be able to move on to Hollywood, he had subtly hinted. She and Mohammad would become "A Listers" on everyone's party invite.

She was pretty sure that she loved Amir, but the lure of stepping onto the first rung of the acting ladder was decisive. She was also a little unsure if her love was reciprocated. Why would Amir want her to meet Mohammad if he loved her so much?

If things didn't work out as planned, she would simply pack her bags and come home.

She heard voices, and instinctively froze, pretending to again be asleep. The pick-up truck's engine was switched off, and everything went silent.

She could hear her heart pounding, and the throbbing pain in her breast and nipples returned. She recognized Mohammad's gentle voice even though he was now speaking in Arabic; the other voices sounded much more intimidating, and commands were being spit out and delivered threateningly.

The door on her side of the pick-up swung open.

Susan froze, and looked straight ahead through the tiny slit in her suffocating black Burka prison.

She felt the hand travelling up her leg – up her thigh – stroking, probing, gently at first, and then becoming ever more animated as it found its target.

'My period Mohammad – tell him about my period.' Susan spoke calmly and quietly, not wanting the filthy swine that was now groping her to hear her English voice. Every fiber in her body wanted to scream. She could feel her stomach churning in revulsion, the bile filling her mouth. She felt an overwhelming hatred burning inside her whole being, as it was constrained and concealed beneath the stinking black strait jacket that Muslim women were forced to wear.

Mohammad spoke to the man in a joking, mocking tone.

The hand was rapidly withdrawn, and held up to show the blood to the rest of the bearded men who were pointing their Kalashnikovs at Mohammad.

Susan heard the laughter.

The pick-up engine was again started, and slowly the vehicle moved forward, Mohammad skillfully winding his way through a maze of burned out vehicles, and several bearded, dust covered men, who were threateningly and mockingly pointing their weapons at him.

'Bloody hell, that was close,' Mohammad said in a much relieved voice – a much relieved Manchester voice. 'I thought that we were gonners that time. There is no way of telling whether they are Shia or Sunni – get it wrong and you are toast.'

'How did you know then? Inside her black tent, Susan was both sweating and curious. She was also filled with an overwhelming urge to kill. Not just Amir, not just the filthy bastard whose hand was now covered in blood, but every stinking, bearded Arab bastard who had buggered and abused her for the last few weeks.

Mohammad glance to his right and smiled. 'To begin with Susan, I thought about flipping a coin, then I noticed a cleric in the background wearing a black turban. Only Shia clerics wear black turbans, so I told them that I was delivering you to a Shia village elder a few miles north near to the Turkish border. If it hadn't been for the blood, you would have been back to square one again, and my arse would probably have been employed as well. It is a very strange religion Susan that allows none stop buggery of young girls and boys, yet cuts off the heads of homosexuals.'

'I thought that shagging young boys meant that you were a homo?'

'Not in the case of the Arabs Susan. They generally live such repressive lives, and having no access to women whatsoever until they are married, buggery is a perfectly acceptable practice. Even after they are married, most men still prefer sticking it in back to front, if you know what I mean. Many of them also prefer the services of young boys to their wives. Make you wonder why there are so many of them really.'

Susan Clarke sat upright, and adjusted the seat on which she had been lying before speaking. 'Where are we Mohammad, and how long have I been asleep for?'

Mohammad smiled, and he let out a chuckle as he spoke. 'Pretty close to the Turkish border, and 7 hours. You have slept every inch of the way. Hopefully we will soon have you back in Leeds in time for the new term at school.'

'I haven't got my passport with me, and when can I get rid of this bloody tent, it's boiling inside here?' Susan lifted the Burka above her knees before remembering that she was wearing no underwear.

She was aware of the blood that was clotting around her thighs – blood that had almost certainly saved her from another bout of physical abuse and buggery.

Mohammad burst out laughing. 'What about the poor women who have to wear them every day of their lives? At least you will be rid of yours in a couple of hours when we reach the convoy.'

'Convoy?'

'A UN aid convoy Susan, everything is in place. That's how we will cross the border, and your new passport is waiting for you at the British Embassy in Istanbul. That is how you arrived in this hell-hole, don't you remember? Amir, your lover, arranged everything.'

'What is going off Mohammad, why all this concern for me? I would have thought that the British Government would have left me here to rot; either that, or get shagged to death. Have you any idea what I have been through these last few days? All of it is your fault. Why were you not at the border to collect me as Amir said?'

Mohammad stroked his bearded chin with his left hand, as he continued driving across the dusty desert road. 'I knew nothing about any meeting that Amir had organized Susan. Do you honestly think that you are the only girl that he has sent over? Did you never wonder how he manages to have such a good lifestyle without doing any work? A big detached house, new BMW car, plus any luxury that he chooses.

You also know nothing about your new found religion. What handsome young Jihadist would marry a girl who wasn't a virgin? If you have been screwing Amir, you can guarantee that he only ever had one thing in mind when he converted you to Islam. I would guess that he earned 20 to 25 grand out of the deal, you're really not that bad looking – well your eyes are OK.' Mohammad burst out laughing, he was well aware that Susan's body was well worth a second glance – he had seriously considered the possibility of indulging himself back at the training camp, but had dismissed all carnal thoughts as soon as he had seen the blood.

'The fucking bastard; what about all those dirty, bearded, stinking Arabs that have been performing every sexual perversion under the sun on me, you mean to say that they have been paying?' Susan Clarke slammed her clenched fist down on the car's dashboard.

'Of course they have,' Mohammad laughed as he spoke. 'I would guess that someone as young and as pretty as you are would be worth at least a camel, or maybe even a couple of goats, in return for ten minutes of your undying love.'

'You bastard.' Beneath the hot and sweaty Burka, Susan Clarke was secretly smiling at the thought of Mohammad standing outside the room shouting "Roll up – roll up. Great shag – only one camel or two goats for ten minutes".

'Anyway Mohammad, you still haven't told me why you are helping me, there must be hundreds, if not thousands of girls from all over the world that are trapped in this hell hole – why me?'

'We need to get to Amir Susan. Other than Saha, you are the only one that knows him well enough.' For the first time, Mohammad's voice had turned serious, almost threatening – the joking, light hearted inflections had evaporated in the hot desert sun.

Susan Clarke suddenly felt uncomfortable. She sensed danger. 'Who are WE Mohammad?' she asked suspiciously. 'And what if I never want to see the bastard again other than to rip his balls off, I can refuse can't I?'

'Of course you can refuse, you will of course be returned to the little love nest where I collected you from, and you will once again become "A Bride for Allah".'

'Please tell me that you are lying Mohammad, I would rather kill myself than go back there.'

'The British intelligence services have put a lot of time in on this one Susan. Amir has been on the terrorist radar for a couple of years now. We have never been able to pin anything on him other than people smuggling, he is much too clever for that. One thing that we do know is that there is something very big being planned, and somehow Amir is at the center of it all. We need you to work with us on this one Susan, we could be looking at another 9/11 here, maybe something even bigger, maybe even involving a nuclear explosion that could kill hundreds of thousands of people.

We also suspect that Amir knows the identity of the British shark. We already know the name of the Middle Eastern one, but we can't even get a sniff of his European counterpart.'

'What does the shark do then?'

'It's just a code name that the secret service uses, they are fond of code names, and think that it makes them sound important. The Saudi shark provides the funding, and the European one arranges and co-ordinates the terrorism. We always thought that most of the terrorism was pretty much 'Lone Wolf' operators, but recently it has become pretty obvious that there is some very sophisticated planning going on. Our intelligence network has always been well on top of the situation until these last few months, now someone is running rings round us, and we haven't got a bloody clue as to who.'

'How do you know that I will be on your side Mohammad, what if I choose to stay Muslim?'

'Here's the bad news Susan, you have to stay Muslim, and you have to once again become friends with Amir. You will have to become an inside operator – a double agent.'

'Is that what you are Mohammad, a double agent for the British Government?' Susan suddenly burst out laughing. 'Oh my god. I'm in the car with James Bond and his Muslim beard, and as for Amir, I would rather kill the bastard than become friends with him again. I have something very special lined up for Amir when the time is right – believe me – something very special.'

Mohammad flashed a serious glance as he turned his head momentarily to face Susan. 'James Bond isn't for real Susan; that is just a film set, no one actually gets hurt. You are not on a film set, you are in a real life situation, and if you don't get it right you will probably die.'

'Then if that is the case, you can stuff your fucking job Mohammad. I have had enough of this religious shit. I have been shagged, buggered, scratched, pinched, and sucked enough dicks to choke a fucking donkey – why should I put my life in danger?' Susan was genuinely angry, and not thinking straight.

'Two reasons,' Mohammad said slowly. 'Number one – you have to get even with Amir, you owe yourself that, and surely you can guess what number two is.'

'Someone will kill me Mohammad?'

Mohammad nodded slowly. Susan Clarke already knew too much. She was either on board with the British intelligence services, or she was to become another casualty of the never ending series of Islamic wars that were constantly being fought over a medieval religion, and an ocean of worthless desert sand.

She closed her eyes and considered her options.

Maybe this would be an opportunity to see just how good she could be as an actress. She could play one side off against the other one. She could become a double agent and still pretend to be Amir's lover, striking when the time was right, striking at a time of her choosing.

She doubted that she could play the role of lover; the thought of Amir sticking his dick in her again filled her with revulsion.

She would have to kiss him and make it look real – feel real.

Maybe – just maybe, acting the part of Amir's lover would be the one sure way of getting close enough to him to ensure that the rest of her plan was feasible.

No – fuck Amir – fuck the British Intelligence Services. She was not going back to Amir.

CHAPTER 5

FREEDOM OF SORTS

'You want me to do what? No bloody way! How can I ever pretend to love that bastard again after what he has put me through? Have you any idea how many times those stinking bastards fucked and buggered me? I can barely stand, let alone walk. Why my arse? Virtually every one of the bastards wanted to stick their dicks in my arse.

No – I am not going back to Amir, I have my own little surprise for that bastard.'

Cathy Taylor and Fiona Watson looked firstly at each other, and then at Mohammad.

Mohammad smiled before speaking.

'Susan, you have no idea what you are dealing with here. Amir is just a little cog in a big wheel. He does however have connections that may eventually lead us to the big operators – the big fish – the sharks. It isn't just about people trafficking; that is just one of the ways that their organization is funded. It is about world terrorism; this is funded and coordinated by the sharks – these are the people that we really want.'

'You said that you would return me to that shithole if I refused to cooperate Mohammad. Were you joking?'

'Of course I was Susan, besides, I always knew that you would come on board; you want to be an actress, now is the perfect opportunity for you to learn your craft.'

'How do you know that?' Susan was suddenly suspicious. 'I never told you that I wanted to be an actress.'

'We have been watching you ever since you first took up with Amir.'

'You knew then that he was sending me to be fucked by those bastards. You knew everything all along – you sat back and did nothing so that you could gather your useless intelligence crap. You fucking bastard Mohammad – you fucking bastard!'

Cathy Taylor interrupted, holding up both hands as she did so, her palms facing Susan. 'Wow Susan, that isn't true. Mohammad was in Syria when you set out for Turkey; you are forgetting that YOU got on the plane, it was your choice, no-one forced you. You were the one that was hoodwinked by Amir; you were the one with the false passport. We had no idea that you were going. If you had used your own passport, we would have stopped you at the airport, and don't forget that Mohammad put his own life in danger by bringing you back.'

Susan Clarke went silent. She was safe now, wrapped and cosseted in and by the British Embassy in Istanbul.

She had bathed, washed, scrubbed – bathed, washed, scrubbed, until her entire body had turned pink.

She still wasn't clean.

Her entire body was a series of black and blue pinch marks. Her nipples were painful to the touch. There were times when she was sure that the dirty, sweaty, stinking bastards were trying to bite them off.

Even without breathing, she could still smell the filth that clung to her entire body – lingering like a rotting piece of fish or meat that was permanently lodged in her nostrils. She could taste the rancid dicks that had choked her and left her gasping for air, as they rhythmically pulled her head into their body. Would the memory ever go away, or would her body forever stink of the sweaty, tobacco tainted, sub human creatures that had invaded her entire body and soul?

'I need another shower. The smell is coming back – I can taste it.' Susan stood up and left the room, slamming the embassy door behind her.

Cathy Taylor and Fiona Watson understood. They realized that Mohammad could not and never would understand. The psychosomatic obsession with stinking, tasting, and the none-stop bathing, were almost always symptomatic of rape victims – more so multiple rape victims. A man could never visualize the long term trauma felt by a woman, or in this case a schoolgirl – a naive 15 year old schoolgirl whose body had been violated, not just the once, but dozens, maybe even hundreds of times. No man could ever understand.

The victims were left unclean, impure. They were soiled and dirty.

Both Cathy and Fiona had dealt with many of the young girls that had been fortunate enough to escape the murderous clutches of the Jihadist; the symptoms were always the same.

Wash, clean, scrub, sanitize, and then repeat the process, again, and then again. The girls could never feel clean – their whole body was poisoned – polluted. It always needed more washing – more purifying.

'Both Cathy and Fiona worked for British intelligence. Their role was mostly Intelligence gathering and analyzing, usually from the returning "Brides of Allah".

Amir not only made money from Rashim when he sold him the girls, he made considerably more when they were returned to their parents. Parents who would often pay vast amounts to have their child back. This usually only occurred when the girls were too pregnant to be of any further use as sex slaves; the bonus windfall being shared equally between Amir and Rashim.

Mohammad was a British secret service field operative with connections. He was also Amir's cousin, and deeply involved with both the British and Syrian Muslim terrorists organizations.

Mohammad lived his life one step away from a mistake – one step away from death. He realized that he was now compromised. There could be no going back to Syria.

Syria was no longer the problem. Amir was now the problem.

'Will she work with us Mohammad?' Cathy asked.

'Yes, I'm pretty sure of that. She is very intelligent; needless to say, she is also very angry. I'm not too sure that we can stop her killing Amir though, she has already talked about drugging him and stuffing his balls into his mouth as I drove her through Syria.'

'Strangely enough, that has been crossing my mind for the whole afternoon,' Fiona laughed as she spoke. 'I haven't been screwed by them, but as she told her story, I could really visualize myself cutting Amir's balls off for setting her up.'

'Wrong modus operandi Fiona,' Cathy grinned as she contributed to the conversation. 'Leave the balls in place so that he still has the urges – just cut the dick off so that he can't satisfy them.'

'I am beginning to feel extremely uncomfortable in your company ladies, so can we please return to sorting Susan out.' Mohammad jokingly visibly shuddered.

Susan Clarke returned some 10 minutes later, her hair still damp, and her face glowing pink. 'I feel much better now, so what is in it for me if I go along with your plan. More to the point, how do I explain to Amir how I escaped from those filthy animals?'

'How about if we guarantee you a place in RADA when you have finished at school?' Cathy Taylor cocked her head to one side as she spoke, and adopted a questioning expression.

> The Royal Academy of Dramatic Art, (RADA) is one of the oldest and most prestigious drama schools in the world, and was founded at the beginning of the twentieth century.

'You can do that?'

'My boss can do anything that he wants to Susan, he has more power than any man in the country, including the Prime Minister.'

Cathy Taylor was not lying.

'What about Amir though, he isn't stupid you know? I have never seen him be violent, he was always the perfect gentleman with me, but the people that he deals with tend to keep a safe distance from him. I've also heard rumors that he has killed people.'

'Why did you go with him then Susan?' Cathy Taylor adopted a questioning facial expression, slightly influenced by the knowledge that she was already aware of the answer.

'Excitement I guess – excitement tinged with a touch of danger.'

Cathy smiled, she had been correct. The hypnotic cocktail of excitement and danger had largely influenced her life's choices.

'Leave Amir to me Susan, I know him better than anyone, we have been dealing together since we were barely teenagers.'

'Selling young girls to be fucked by filthy Arabs Mohammad?'

The expression on Mohammad's face turned momentarily to one of anger as he spoke. 'You are out of line there Susan, I put MY life on the line to get you out of Syria.' His expression and voice suddenly softened. 'Any more comments like that, and I will personally drive you back to Allah's love palace and sell you to the highest bidder. If Rashim can get a camel for ten passionate minutes of your time, I should be able to get an entire camel caravan for completely off-loading you.'

'Bastard.' All 3 girls were laughing, as Susan raised two fingers in Mohammad's direction.

'I said, I will deal with Amir, he trusts me.'

Susan Clarke wasn't so sure. Mohammad may well be his cousin, but she had seen the fear in peoples' eyes whenever they had dealt with Amir. There was just something about him that she was very wary of. He had only ever been loving and tender towards her, but, there was still something about his persona that inspired caution – a latent, invisible, malicious intent – controlled, but never caged.

She had ignored this when in his presence, the true nature only becoming apparent as she had viewed him through the portal – the only mental escape route that she had been able to visualize during the weeks of abuse.

Amir had been blocking the portal – preventing her from mentally leaving the room – keeping her mind, body, and soul captive.

The eyes held hidden secrets – hidden powers – hidden threats.

It would take an exceptionally good actress to disguise the hatred concealed behind HER eyes.

She would be that exceptionally good actress, but only in the short term. Her long term plans for Amir were somewhat different.

Fuck Mohammad – Fuck Amir – Fuck Allah.

Susan Clarke would be working to her own agenda.

She would be making her move at a time of her choosing.

CHAPTER 6

ON TV

Amir and Saha were sat together on the larger of the two settees in Amir's expensive and spacious detached house, in one of Leeds' wealthier and more up-market suburbs. They were watching the BBC news with both excitement and cruel satisfaction.

Amir was aware of the rather too close proximity of Saha, but was not concerned; he had just received close on 50 grand; '50 bloody great smackers,' he had called them in his Leeds accent, for the footage of the bus crash, which was now showing across the world on every TV news channel. The sight of schoolchildren, both boys and girls, screaming, and trying to escape the burning inferno had tripled, maybe even quadrupled the little silver disc's value.

This was turning into a highly profitable couple of months. Amir's Middle Eastern bank-balance had been swelled by 50 grand from the Arab TV company, and 20 from the sale of the girl. He felt a little guilty over Susan though; he really liked her, not enough to turn down the 20 grand of course, but she had been a virgin when he had first met her, which in itself set her out as rather special in a city like Leeds.

He would soon find another vulnerable young girl, trick her into falling in love with him, and then introduce her to Allah. The whole process usually took around 2 or 3 months, then it was good bye, good luck, and hello 20 grand. This amount could easily be doubled for a 10 or 11 year old virgin. Amir had furnished Allah with many brides.

His easier targets were the bad girls; young girls who were on the at risk register, the ones under the care of the council, the ones in the special schools reserved for delinquents. These young 11 and 12 year olds were like putty in his hands. A few rides in his shiny new BMW, a few glasses of vodka, the odd snort of coke, and as soon as the precautionary fake passport was sorted, he passed them on to the "export" department of his operation, as he liked to call it.

Lilly white Infidel girls, so young, were highly prized throughout the Arab world, and would often command as much as 30 grand if they were still virgins. These girls were often sold directly to rich merchants, or even to the Middle Eastern Royal families, if their youth and virginity was accompanied by beauty.

The authorities rarely followed up the disappearance of these at risk girls, knowing that they would be off and away at the first opportunity; disappearing into the twilight world of child prostitution at the hands of the Pakistani and Arab communities.

The Prophet Mohammad had consummated his marriage to his 6 year old bride, Aisha, when she had turned 9, so the morality of the Western World was unimportant to Muslims – of no consequence what so ever.

Good Muslims lived their lives in the image of the Prophet, not British or European law. The law of the land was irrelevant – the law of Allah – Sharia Law, was all they understood and followed.

Not all the girls were prepared to follow Amir's plans; the problem however was not insurmountable. One single tablet of Rohypnol, and the drugged girl became 100% compliant – her next recollection in life being of lying under some hot, bearded, sweaty Arab in the Middle East, as he filled her with Arab semen – and made her "A Bride for Allah".

Yes, God was truly great; Amir had probably the most lucrative business in the North of England, with a never ending supply of fresh young virgins – Allahu Akbar.

The doorbell rang, just as the best part of the bus accident was about to appear for the 5th time on Amir's TV. This was the moment where Sam Stevens leaps from his empty bus and tries to save his son from the blazing inferno of the school bus, before being completely engulfed by fire, and then blown apart by a further explosion.

This was pure Hollywood, Amir couldn't have scripted anything so dramatic; surely he sold the disc much too cheaply? So far, the Arab TV company must have made millions from the disc – the footage was now being shown all over the world, and all he had to show for it was a lousy 50 grand.

It was a great pity that he couldn't agree a price before they arranged the accident; that way they could put it out to tender and take commission on all subsequent sales and repeats. Amir smiled at the thought of such an absurdity.

Was it an absurdity?

Since Saha had managed to clone his school professor's computer, nothing seemed to be beyond him. He may not be able to control time itself, but he could control future events – he could virtually control future time. No computer was outside of his control – traffic lights – railway signals, even the air traffic controller's computer system could be instructed to give a false reading.

Amir's photography had been poor as the cargo plane had crashed into the Manchester airport hangar. The choice of planes had also been poor as few people had died. The more people that died – the greater the pay day. Amir had learned this lesson well, that was why he had chosen a bus packed with school children.

The doorbell rang again. Amir flicked his head in the direction of the door, and Saha arose like the faithful lap dog that he was to answer it, letting out a gasp at the sight of Mohammad and Susan; the same Susan who only a few weeks before had been on her way to become "A Bride for Allah".

Amir arose to greet the couple, and throwing his arms around Mohammad, almost shouted in mock delight, 'Cousin Mohammad, welcome back to my humble abode, and thank you for returning my Susan to me.'

Both men burst out laughing. Amir's home was anything but humble, and had been visited by Mohammad on many occasions.

Susan Clarke almost recoiled in revulsion as Amir wrapped her in a hug, holding on to her for almost half a minute, stroking her hair, and gently kissing her on her cheek.

Her eyes involuntarily settled on a large silver kitchen knife that was lying on the small table sat between Amir's two large, expensive, cream settees, alongside a couple of apples. She felt an almost overwhelming urge to plunge the knife deep into Amir's lying throat and mouth, but she had been well schooled by the efficient Cathy and Fiona, whilst still at the British Embassy in Istanbul. Susan Clarke was a quick learner; she was also on a mission of her own – a mission of revenge. What she had got planned for Amir would be far more satisfying than the instant death at the hands of a kitchen knife.

It had been difficult arranging a plausible reason for Mohammad's rescue of Susan. They had only ever met a couple of times before at the Mosque where Amir had first radicalized her, and on each occasion, she had been wearing her Burka. Only her beautiful, mesmeric blue eyes; eyes that flashed flecks of sapphire, and hints of opal, had been visible, so why would he choose

Susan over the hundreds, perhaps even thousands, of young, white, Islamic sex slaves who were now trapped throughout the Middle East?

'I did it for you Amir,' Mohammad said. 'When I went to meet Rashim, I recognized her immediately. No one could ever forget those eyes. She was almost delirious, and would only repeat one word – Amir. As soon as she could speak rationally, she begged me to bring her home, so I tricked Rashim and returned her to you. Are you not pleased cousin? Allah has blessed you both. I fear that I will be of little use to you in Syria now, Rashim will certainly kill me the moment that I return.'

Amir looked genuinely pleased – not so Saha.

Saha felt nothing but jealousy and contempt for Susan, he was also suspicious. A random meeting such as Mohammad had just described, went against all the mathematical laws of probability. She was also an Infidel, not worthy of being "A Bride for Allah"; her conversion would never be recognized by any serious Muslim. The clerics talked about her at the Mosque. They knew what Amir's plans were for her, but were genuinely fearful of upsetting him. Amir carried considerable presence throughout the Leeds Muslim community; it was a fearful presence, and was well left alone.

He would ask Mr. Bean's computer to check up on Mohammad. Mr. Bean's computer seemed to know everything. It seemed to have a mind of its own. It could think. No matter what he asked it, it always came up with the right answer. How did it do that? No other computer in the world could be programmed to do what Mr. Bean's computer could do.

Saha's attention returned to the television, where once again, Sam Stevens was about to be blown to pieces thanks to Mr. Bean's computer.

CHAPTER 7

SCRIPTED

Professor Jeremy Blythe sat watching the Leeds Bus disaster unfold on his TV in the comfort of his own home, with Fido sat on his lap. Something most certainly did not seem right.

Why did the camera move from bus to bus, as they both approached the traffic lights? It was just like watching an action movie. It was a written script surely – an extremely well written script.

The whole sequence of events added to the build-up of tension. Each scripted event was followed by the professional camera work that recorded the initial crash between the two buses, and then the massive explosion at the petrol station.

The movie moved on – from tension, through to exhilarating action, and then on to horror, with the images of screaming children clawing at the bus windows, only to be consumed by the fire and a further series of explosions.

Enter the movie hero – for a while it looked as if Sam Stevens had arrived in the nick of time, and would rescue the trapped children, as he in turn clawed away at the door of the blazing bus – then – it all went horribly wrong.

A massive explosion blew him to pieces.

This is where the whole scenario moved away from an action movie, into the surrealistic world of indescribable, unacceptable reality – everyone died – even the hero.

Heroes don't die in the movies.

They had got the script wrong – there had been a big mistake – where was the happy ending?

Someone needed to be sacked.

What kind of person would concentrate a camera on infants with their hair and clothes ablaze instead of trying to save them?

This would never happen in a movie; people are much too sensitive; it would be banned, binned, and the director would never work again.

Blythe's mind flashed back to the two young men that he had seen walking away from the disaster, one of them, the older and much taller of the two, had been sporting a fairly substantial Muslim type beard; not so the younger one, he had only caught a fleeting glimpse, yet something about him definitely looked familiar. He was walking with an ungainly stoop. He almost looked deformed.

It had to be Saha.

The walk had been the awkward gait of a boy with no athletic prowess whatsoever. A boy who avoided all forms of physical sport. A boy whose physical development was not only stunted, but seemed to have come to a complete halt – an under developed boy whose communicative and assimilation skills were still barely at a junior grade level.

Saha simply did not fit into any category of pupil that could be profiled.

Saha did not belong – he barely existed – he was inconsequential – he may have been there in body, but he was never really there.

He was an intellectual presence that appeared to exist on the outer fringes of nothing and nowhere.

The British intelligence services were also suspicious at the news flashes that were by now covering the globe.

Over the last few months, there had been a series of unexplained disasters in the country, and somehow, they always seemed to have been caught by an anonymous camera man, and shown by most of the world's press.

There was a sophisticated distribution network involved, and someone was making a lot of money out of these disasters, yet, with the finest computer brains in the country at their disposal, no cyber trail of money could be located, let alone followed. What the authorities and the security services did know however, was that most of the footage was being distributed by someone in the Middle East; at that point, the trail went cold.

With access to one of the world's only 3 super computers in existence, it was simply inconceivable that any financial transaction could take place anywhere in the world that could not be pin-pointed and isolated.

There was no cyber trail – none. Not even a hint or a whiff of any form of financial transaction ever taking place.

British Intelligence was completely baffled.

Surely, no one would distribute such valuable material for free. What would be the point?

If the distribution was from the Middle East, then the financial dealings were almost certainly being done in that region of the world, and were probably finding their way into the hands of the Islamic terrorists' organizations.

Horror was being used to finance terror.

CHAPTER 8

A GRAVE FOR MOHAMMAD

Mohammad left Amir's home fairly late in the evening, leaving Susan to make her own way home by Taxi. He had things to do and people to meet.

As the taxi arrived, Amir had looked deeply into Susan's eyes, the intention being quite obvious. Susan shook her head as she spoke. 'Sorry Amir, I am still waiting for all the test results from the hospital, you really have no idea what you put me through. You promised me that Mohammad would be waiting for me at the Turkish border, the only thing waiting was a dirty, filthy, middle aged bastard that stunk of goats. From there I was taken to a bombed out town where I was abused almost nonstop for weeks. Do you really want to take a chance on catching aids, hepatitis, gonorrhea, syphilis? I have been tested for the bloody lot. I didn't think that a shag could carry so many diseases. The only good thing I know so far is that I am not pregnant.'

Susan climbed into the waiting taxi, and recoiled as the driver's Arabic appearance was highlighted by a nearby street lamp.

She suddenly felt the sick rising from her stomach, as visions of the endless abuse flashed before her; the smell of rotting fish and meat invaded her senses.

The actress put in an appearance. She offered a seemingly genuine smile to Amir.

Susan Clarke was good. One day she would be famous. Before that however, she would deal with Amir when the time was right.

Amir spoke in Arabic to the taxi driver, and handed over a ten pound note, blowing a kiss as the taxi departed.

'You know that this is a set up Amir,' Saha said, as Amir re-entered the house and closed the door. 'I don't know if the girl is involved, but Mohammad is hiding something. Mr. Bean's computer told me that Mohammad was in Istanbul for 6 days. Why would he do that? He has never spent more than one night there.'

'How would the computer know that Saha? Mohammad is so careful, he only uses cash wherever he travels; his credit cards are used in either Leeds or Manchester by his UK associates whenever he is away on business, and his false passport has fooled the authorities for years.'

'Facial recognition Amir. Mr. Bean's computer searched every CCTV memory bank in Turkey; garages, hotels, even street cameras', he was there for 6 days and 5 nights. Mr. Bean's computer is never wrong.

I have been in touch with Rashim. He is furious, and is demanding his money back. Mohammad can never go back to Syria. He will be beheaded the moment that he sets foot in the country. The girl was making a lot of money for Rashim, and now he is worried that the whole business is in danger of being discovered. What if Mohammad is working for the authorities? He knows too much and must be killed.'

'Tomorrow Saha, we will take care of the matter,' Amir sounded serious yet reluctant. 'I will not harm the girl though. Let Rashim know that I will send him a replacement free of charge in a couple of weeks; my business associates in Bradford and Keighley will be delivering 4 fresh young virgins shortly. Rashim will be well pleased. Tonight though, we have a grave to dig. You are of course correct about Mohammad, his lies were written all over his face. Mohammad is a traitor to Allah, and a danger to our future plans.'

Saha burst out laughing before speaking. 'How long has Jihada John been a business associate Amir? You forget that it is me that you are speaking to, not the Imams at the Mosque.'

Amir grinned as he cuffed the back of Saha's head.

As agreed the previous evening, Mohammad arrived at Amir's house at dusk. From there, they were to go on to the Mosque for evening prayers, and to arrange a price for the transportation of the 4 young virgins.

Rashim had demanded 2 of them free of charge; Susan had been earning him lots of money, and was in big demand from all his fighters. Amir had told him only one - only one it was. Few people went against Amir. Even a man as powerful and as dangerously violent as Rashim knew that Amir had both money and connections, and in a land where a human life has less value than that of a goat or a camel, it was sensible to do business without making unnecessary enemies. There were enough enemies in this land - enemies of the same religion - enemies that read and adhered to the same messages contained in the same Quran - enemies that had aligned themselves with the cursed Americans and the animal Jews.

Mohammad was to accompany the girls to the Turkish border with Syria, and to administer the necessary tranquilizing drugs to each of them when necessary. At the border, they would be handed over to Rashim.

Mohammad was unsure of the reception he would receive from Rashim; still, even if he had taken his prized girl, he was replacing her free of charge with a younger one.

He decided not to take any chances with Rashim – he did not trust him. Rashim had been a warlord in his native Afghanistan before moving to Syria, and there was still a good price on his head – dead or alive. He had killed many Americans, and they wanted revenge.

When the time was right, he would make the necessary arrangements with the Americans, but as a British operative, his current mission was to lure the Middle Eastern shark to within range of the American guns.

They had to cut off the Saudi funding for world-wide terrorism.

The current crop of young virgins were the bait.

All 3 of them entered Amir's spacious double garage through a door in the kitchen, and as Mohammad bent his back and head forward in order to climb into the back seat of the BMW, Amir plunged the long, sharpened screw driver into his ear and deep into his brain, shaking his hand around from side to side in order to ensure ever more effectiveness. The screw driver was then rapidly withdrawn, the grooves and mini barbs cut into it dragging out bloodied portions of brain. Death was immediate.

Mohammad's limp body slumped to the garage floor, and involuntary continued twitching for a couple of minutes. The flow of blood was minor, and immediately stopped as Saha pushed a rag into his ear. This was not the first time that Amir's garage had been used as an execution chamber. People who crossed Amir often disappeared. The people at the Leeds' Mosque were both aware and wary of this.

A journey of little more than 40 minutes saw Mohammad's lifeless body unceremoniously dumped into the shallow grave that Saha had dug the previous evening. Amir stood guard as Saha covered the body with soil.

Mohammad would now be forever sleeping on Saddleworth Moor with the child victims of Hindley and Brady.

'I told you that he was a traitor Amir, Mr. Bean's computer never lies,' Saha looked pleased with himself as he flattened out the soil now covering Mohammad. 'Tonight, many more infidels will be joining him.'

Amir felt a deep sense of guilt at killing his cousin. They had been friend for many years, and their family connections went back many generations, way beyond Leeds; back to their homeland in the Middle East. He was not totally convinced that his cousin was a traitor to the cause no matter what Saha's damned computer had told him, but he could not afford to take any chances. When asked, Mohammad had told him that he had only stayed in Istanbul for one night – Mr. Bean's computer had told Saha that he had stayed for 6 days and 5 nights. Why would a computer lie? 'Could a computer lie?' Amir wondered.

What Amir and Saha were working on dwarfed any act of terrorism that had ever been seen on the planet before. The destruction of the Twin Towers in New York had seen a couple of thousand Infidels killed; their plan could even top a couple of billion. Of course there would be Muslim casualties, but Allah would understand.

Allah would be waiting to honor Amir in Paradise. Amir genuinely hoped that Allah would have something nice planned for Saha – he didn't really have a life here on earth.

CHAPTER 9

RATIONAL DOUBTS

As Amir lay in bed that evening, his mind was in turmoil. He was beginning to harbor doubts about their embryonic planned sacrifice to Allah.

Just supposing that Allah didn't really exist.

There were too many unanswered questions beginning to flood his mind. The Christian friends that he knew had long ago dismissed the idea of any supreme being; to them, there was no God, nor was there any after-life. You simply died and ceased to exist.

Ashes to Ashes – Dust to Dust.

Amir knew all about Charles Darwin. Just supposing that he had been right. Maybe we did simply evolve. Why should the Quran be any more right than Darwin's "Origin of species" simply because some bitter old cleric had told him so?

Evolution or creation?

If Allah had created mankind out of a single clot of blood, where then did the blood come from? Why not simply cut out the middle-man? A smile crossed his half sleeping face.

Images of Mohammad and Senta flashed before his eyes; his mind and thoughts wondered why Islam always ended up killing people. There was never any mention of the good things in life wherever you looked in the Quran – only violence – only killing.

Kill the Jews – kill the homosexuals – kill the adulteresses – kill the infidels.

This was touted as a religion of peace.

Hitler's Mein Kampf was a benign fairy story in comparison to the Quran, and it contained less anti-semitism.

Why had Allah allowed him to fall in love with an infidel girl? He was aware that she had never become a committed Muslim, and had only accepted the faith because of his persuasion.

Why had his lifelong friend Senta been persuaded to blow himself to pieces at the football match only 8 weeks earlier?

What had all those young children who were stood close to Senta at the Elland Road stadium done to offend Allah? They had never bombed the Mosques – they had never killed Muslims – they had never disrespected Allah or the Prophet.

Amir and Senta loved football, and had been avid Leeds United fans since primary school, so why didn't that old bastard Imam at the Mosque choose another ground? He had convinced Senta that it would prove beyond doubt that his one and only true love was his devotion to Allah and the Prophet.

This was beginning to sound like bullshit.

If such an action guaranteed Senta a place in Paradise, would he really remain forever young and have 72 beautiful young virgins? Where was the evidence – where was the proof? He only had a dying old man's word for it.

Why didn't the arthritic old cleric at the Mosque who had promised him all of this go to the football match and blow himself up? Surely an instant placement in Paradise was much better that the slow lingering death that the terminal cancer eating away at his insides offered him?

Did the cleric himself doubt the existence of both Allah and Paradise? There could be no other reason or explanation.

There were also many contradictions in the Quran itself. Why did the Archangel Gabriel convey Allah's message to the Prophet; what was wrong with Allah speaking to him directly, didn't he trust him?

Why was it that every civilization since time began, had worshipped one or more different Gods? Was it reasonable to assume that every one of them had been wrong, and only Allah was the right one?

The choice of Allah by the Prophet Mohammad had been a little like sticking a pin in a book of names in order to name a child. There had been 360 Pagan Gods available to Mohammad, so why did he chose Allah and then discard the other 359?

Allah had been a Pagan Moon God – why not choose a Sun God? Surely the sun is more important than the moon; not that he ever saw much of either in Leeds.

If by good fortune, Mohammad had stuck the pin in the correct name, and considering that Islam has only been around for less than 1400 years, it would mean that of the trillions of people who had lived over the last 200,000 years, none of them had gone to heaven or Paradise, simply because they were not Muslim.

This then meant that Paradise did not exist until long after the Prophet had been born; so either Allah, or the Prophet, must have created Paradise 1400 years ago. If the Earth has been around for billions of years, why did Paradise take so long in its' creation?

Did Allah create Paradise as an after-thought?

Did the Islamic Mullahs and Imams invent Paradise simply as a means of controlling the masses, and as a way of persuading immature and brainwashed young minds into becoming make believe martyrs simply for political purposes?

Was religion really the opium of the people, as Karl Marx had once described it?

Before he finally dropped off to sleep, Amir amused himself by imagining Allah searching Leeds for 72 virgins. Sometimes the 11 and 12 year olds that he shipped out to Rashim had lost much of their value long before he acquired them.

This emphasis on virgins puzzled him. Although he had slept with many women over the last few years, Susan had been the only virgin, and the first time had been pretty horrible.

Susan had been so nervous that his own performance was definitely not up to scratch, and the blood had lead to him destroying all the bed linen.

If the attraction was in the fact that the girls were virgins, did this mean that in Paradise, they healed themselves after each session?

Did the virgins in Paradise bleed as Susan had done?

How many sets of bed linen did Senta need in Paradise?

How many virgins did he now have left before he run out?

What then? Would they be replaced by 72 more?

Could they get pregnant?

His half sleeping face broke into a big grin. Who would wash and clean all the nappies, or did they use disposable nappies in Paradise?

Did he give the girls numbers, and keep records so that he could service them all in order?

Did he now have 72 mothers in law to contend with?

He again smiled at the thought of Senta eating 3 square meals of Viagra and chips every day, and of him rubbing ointment on his sore dick.

Amir was aware that he had to keep his religious doubts to himself. There was no doubting Saha's commitment to the faith, and no way must

Saha ever think that he was himself doubting the validity and existence of Allah.

It would probably be a good idea to put their master plan on hold. Amir now had an enviable and financially rewarding lifestyle. He also had the grudging respect of both his peers and his elders.

He was also falling very much in love.

Surely Allah would be willing to wait?

Life was much too good at the moment, and he was quite content with his own little none virgin. The rest of the girls would just have to wait for him in Paradise until he was ready.

'Be patient little virgins.' He muttered out loud, before finally falling into a deep sleep.

CHAPTER 10

THE MEETING

The Prime minister of Britain was nervously awaiting the arrival of his most senior Intelligence chiefs.

What the hell was happening to his country, and on his watch? He had already doubled the budget for the anti-terrorism department of his administration, so how could so many bombs have exploded all on the same night?

There had seemed to be no logical pattern to the damned thing. London, being the capital city, had almost always been the target, even during the malevolent IRA bombing campaign, yet the previous evening had seen explosions in many of Britain's major cities. Unlike previous terrorist events however, where the objective had always been to cause as many civilian casualties as possible, these explosions seemed to have targeted individual houses, many of them destroying whole families. In total, upwards of 30 children had died.

Strangely, none of the explosions could be attributed to suicide bombings.

Muslims generally preferred to be suicide bombers.

Becoming a martyr guaranteed their ascent to Paradise.

There was a knock on the door, and the PM's personal secretary popped her head round. 'They are here sir,' she said.

'Thank you Samantha, please show them in.'

The 3 most senior members of the intelligence service, and the Home Secretary walked into the room, each one of them sporting glum and worried expressions.

'Where is Peter?' Daniel Hawkins, the British Prime Minister broke into a big grin as he spoke. 'He usually can't wait to get to me and demand more money for his department. Has he been delayed, or has he decided to commit Hara-kiri because the Treasury won't allow him to have any more money until after the next budget?'

The PM suddenly realized the folly of his light hearted remarks; one look at the other men's faces told him all. He immediately regretted his flippancy.

'I'm afraid that Peter was one of the bomb victims last night Prime Minister, together with his entire family.' The words were spoken in a very solemn manner by Sir Cecil Frodsham, the most senior of the intelligence men; a man in over-all control of Britain's vast anti-terrorism expenditure; a man so powerful, it was rumored that even the Home Secretary touched his forelock when addressed – a man so powerful that people opposing him often met with unfortunate accidents, occasionally disappearing without trace. No one now opposed Sir Cecil Frodsham.

'Sorry,' said the PM, his face sporting a chastened expression, and his cheeks momentarily flushing lightly pink. 'I had no idea.'

'It wasn't just Peter, Prime Minister,' Frodsham said. 'It was every senior undercover operative that we had on the ground in the entire country. Someone has hacked into our personnel files and discovered the names and addresses of everyone involved in this ongoing Muslim problem – now we are completely blind, and virtually starting our anti-terrorism department from scratch. Everything, and I do mean everything, has been erased. Our records are like looking at a blank page – we no longer have any records.'

'It had to have been planned for weeks,' offered the Home Secretary. 'Every explosion happened at exactly the same time.'

The Prime Minister was more concerned with the intelligence implications than the loss of the operatives – they could be replaced.

'What about back up Cecil?' The PM looked incredulous, and could feel his anger rising. 'You are working on a budget of millions, surely you have back up, your computer is one of the three most powerful computers in the world, and your computer software system alone cost more than the GDP of some African countries?'

'Of course we do sir, or at least we did. Somehow, a virus has entered our back up system and has wiped out everything that we have been storing for many years. My computer boffins' tell me that it would be impossible for a human brain to devise and create such a virus, the system was deemed completely foolproof. They also tell me that of the 3 super computers in the world that could be so utilized, 2 of them are operated by the American military, and my department has total control over the third one. There is no way that the Americans would sabotage our systems as their national security is so interlinked with our own.'

'Nothing is impossible Cecil.' For some strange reason, the PM found himself smiling, as his mind travelled back in time to a young man who had made the seemingly impossible suddenly become possible.

'I know of such a brain Cecil, a human super computer, my old mate Jeremy Blythe. I believe that he is a school teacher now at some nondescript Northern Comprehensive. We were at Cambridge together 30 or so years ago. Jeremy possesses such a brain, believe me, he simply has no ambition to put it to any use other than teaching an uninterested bunch of school kids. It's such a bloody waste if you ask me. A brain as colossally complex, and with the ingenuity of Jeremy's, should be put to use for the good of mankind. Jeremy would probably make your multi-million pound super computer blush with embarrassment if he were to put his mind to it.'

'I have some pretty smart people on my books Prime Minister, almost all of them are Oxbridge graduates. I chose them myself, and I doubt that a school teacher would be in their league.' Sir Cecil Frodsham initially sounded hurt, and moved over to the offensive as he spoke.

Frodsham hated to be challenged on any matter. His word was the law. How dare Hawkins compare a school teacher with his own hand-picked subordinates; that was simply disrespectful, and sent out all the wrong messages to the other people in the room: Frodsham's alter-ego often thought of itself as omnipotent.

'I'm sure you have Cecil, but believe me when I tell you, Jeremy Blythe operates in a different dimension to your average graduate. The university lecturers used to shake their heads in disbelief at his mental ability and powers of reasoning. Jeremy Blythe lives in a world that will be 100 years in the future of our world; the last time I looked him up, some ten or so years ago, he was in the process of creating a computer that would design, and self-program both itself and other computers, if you know what I mean. Much too advanced for my brain to grasp, nevertheless, a pretty dangerous concept if you ask me. Who the hell knows where that will lead if we no longer have control over the damned things?

Anyway Cecil, tell me about the casualties from last night. I thought that we had broken the back of this problem when we locked up those bearded bastards from Luton last month. Finally, we seem to have found a judge that has used some common sense. 20 years is not a day too soon for them, and if I had my way, they would be fed nothing but bacon sandwiches and pork chops, and I would have their heads and beards shaved every day for their entire sentence.'

'I agree Prime Minister, and I will be pushing for similar sentences for anyone even thinking about a terrorist event.' George Halton, the Home Secretary broke his silence again in his obvious pursuit of favor and brownie points.

The rest of the Parliamentary cabinet had little time for the Home Secretary, considering him to be no more than a yes man – a poodle to be lead around on the end of the PM's leash. Unknown to them however, this had been the PM's reason for appointing George Halton to the much coveted post. The PM may not as yet have over emphasized his aggressive anti-Islamic agenda, so much as an anti-terrorism policy, but he most certainly knew where his gut feeling would eventually lead him and the rest of the country. He also knew that he could most certainly count on the support of his pet poodle.

'I will of course back you to the hilt on that one George, but tread warily, we cannot be seen to be infringing on the "Human Rights" of half a dozen terrorists in order to protect a few million civilians.' The PM shook his head and smiled. 'Anyway Cecil, tell me all there is to know about last night's bombings. How exposed are we now? Can we still counter the Islamic threat from within our borders? We are still some way in front of the French and Swedes, and it is your job to make sure that it remains that way.'

Sir Cecil Frodsham began to reel off a list of names who had perished in the previous evening's bombings, together with their special undercover functions. In all, 16 highly skilled operatives who had been living and working amongst their local Muslim communities, together with most of their families, had been blown up, and in some cases burned alive. Two had managed to escape with no more than minor injuries, and their Leeds and Manchester operative appeared to have gone to ground.

'How many does that leave Cecil?' the PM asked. 'Just how exposed are we?'

'None sir,' came the reply. 'Not one single operative that was working undercover within the Islamic community is alive, other than the two that escaped the bombs, and the one that has gone missing in Leeds. The 3 of them are now useless to us of course as their cover has been completely blown. As you know sir, Peter was their link with the rest of the security departments; that is almost certainly why he was targeted.'

'How bloody big is their network Cecil?' The PM was shaking his head as he spoke. 'And how are they all interlinked? To arrange an event such as last night would take far more than a Rag Tag army of terrorists operating independently. This would have required the coordination and planning of some seriously clever people, particularly without your department being able to detect it. Surely you must have noticed something, perhaps an increase or slight variation in the internet traffic, not just here, but throughout the Muslim world?'

'That's the most worrying part sir,' Frodsham scratched his head as he continued. 'We have computers that can detect the slightest anomaly in internet traffic; every key word is scrutinized and investigated. A similar message that was transmitted to 20 bombers would set every alarm bell ringing. It would never escape us, it would be totally impossible, we are all completely baffled, our cyber screening is 100 % foolproof.'

'Ok then gentlemen,' the PM was both anxious and angry at the way things were going, after all, during his election campaign, it was he who had stolen the thunder from his political rivals by promising new and almost draconian measures and laws against the terrorists. 'I want to see you all in a couple of days at the same time – and Cecil?'

'Yes sir.'

'Kindly bring along Killgary, your perpetually angry top computer boffin.'

'Glengarry sir.' Frodsham smiled a knowing smile. For some inexplicable reason, the PM often called him Killgary. Glengarry hated it. Daniel Hawkins had an exceptional memory and forgot little, so he obviously took delight in angering one of the most unpleasant men in Government service.

'I am going to locate my boffin and I will be bringing him along to the meeting. Prepare yourselves for a rough ride gentlemen, I doubt that you have ever been in the presence of genius before, believe me, very soon you will be. And one more thing gentlemen; there must be no further correspondence on security matters that goes through the normal channels. It would appear that someone is listening in to the people who are supposed to be listening in to them. For all we know, WE, gentlemen, may well be the next targets – George.'

'Yes sir?'

'I want you to liaise with Cecil and his department on personal security. Double up on security personnel, and call in a few of the top military specialists from Hereford. I want all cabinet members covered by the SAS until further notice; civilian clothing only. Instruct all cabinet members that all none essential future engagements are cancelled, and they are to travel nowhere without security, not even to the corner shop. Make sure that their homes are covered as well – wall to wall 24 hour surveillance.'

'It's done sir.'

'Thank you George. I have now got to go and face the world's press. What am I supposed to say to them? Sorry chaps, but we haven't got a bloody clue who did it, neither do we have any bloody chance of finding out, as my security services have misplaced all their bloody files.'

The PM's voice was laced with sarcasm. Three men in the room stared uncomfortably straight ahead, their faces betraying no emotion.

The Home secretary smiled.

Seeing the smile, Sir Cecil Frodsham's blank expression turning into an angry glare.

With that, Prime Minister Daniel Hawkins rose purposefully from his seat, to be respectfully followed by the other 4 men. He shook the hand of each man in turn before walking towards the door, pausing and turning round to face them as he spoke. 'I don't know where the recent events are leading us gentlemen, but I fear the worst. We appear to be confronted by an enemy whose intelligence, ingenuity, and ruthlessness, are increasing exponentially, and now, we don't even know who they are, or where they are.

Churchill warned the country about the danger of Islam in 1899, and no one listened – Enoch Powell warned the country about unlimited immigration in the sixties, and it cost him his career – I warned the fucking country about the rise of Islam over ten years ago, and it nearly cost me my career. Maybe they will listen now before it is too late, and we all have to grow beards and worship some mythical Middle Eastern Father Christmas and his never ending supply of virgins. Where is he finding all these bloody virgins, that's what I want to know, it certainly isn't in this country?'

The four men smiled as the PM left the room.

'Where exactly WAS Allah finding all these virgins? So far, the figures numbered many thousands, and these were only the British virgins;

what about the rest of Europe? Every country was suffering the same Islamic problems as Britain – France and Sweden doubly so.

Suicide bombing seemed to have become the national sport of every young Muslim man and woman throughout the European continent.

CHAPTER 11

A RATIONAL FEAR

France had a far greater number of Muslims than Britain, second proportionally only to Sweden. Sweden was now a lost cause in the fight against Islamic terrorism. Decades of virtually unregulated inward immigration had seen the imposition of Sharia law throughout the Muslim ghettos.

The government had never voted in Sharia law – the Muslim community had simply unilaterally declared it for all Muslims, and were now agitating for its implementation, by law, for ALL Swedish citizens.

The Swedish military were on standby – Civil War was a hair's breadth away.

The rest of Europe looked on.

This was the inevitably future for the continent, the problem having been multiplied many time over by the disastrous decision of Angela Merkels, the German Chancellor, to welcome, and metaphorically open the floodgates to millions of Muslim immigrants, who unable to believe their luck, immediately packed their bags, and set out for the promised lands of Europe.

Only the military now stood between total submission to Allah and religious freedom. The civilian authorities had neither the manpower nor the firepower to hold their own against the rising tide of Islam.

Prime Minister Daniel Hawkins was a realist, and could see that unless the Western World stood up to Islam, it would have to submit to Islam. The very word itself means submission

Daniel Hawkins submitted to no one.

Not only was Daniel Hawkins tall and well built, but in his younger days he had been extremely handy with his fists – often a little too handy and too impetuous. In any form of confrontation, be it physical or verbal, he never once took a backwards step; not necessarily something that you would associate with a man who had obtained a first at Cambridge with consummate ease. Never the less, he was not a man to push around – not even gently.

He had been extremely intolerant of Islam during his Cambridge days, occasionally resolving over-zealous and over animated opponents' arguments with a resigned shrug of his shoulders – before knocking them out.

Daniel Hawkins refused to take a backward step, and couldn't see any point in trying to make a point to someone who wasn't prepared to listen.

He had realized at an early age that there was no point in preaching to the Islamic converted – force was the only answer – not reasoned argument – not laws – simply force, and in the context of the nation, that meant military force.

Twelve years earlier, he had tried to enter Parliament on an anti-Islamic platform, and had been rounded on by the left wing Liberal press and the BBC.

Within 2 years, the British people had begun to wake up from their comfortable Islamic acceptance and compliance.

Multicultural dreams were turning into blood soaked nightmarish realities.

The British television companies didn't like to show blood – that would upset people.

Foreign television companies enjoyed showing blood.

Internet access now allowed the British people to see the reality of what was happening to their once green and pleasant land – it was turning red – blood red.

Images of body parts – severed heads – blood spattered children and collapsed churches invaded the British peoples' living rooms.

Daniel Hawkins had warned the British people about this all those years ago. Why had they allowed the left wing, Liberal, politically correct fools to crucify him?

Islamic terrorism in its many forms now stalked the streets of Britain, and like a virulent cancer, was beginning to invade every aspect of British life.

Daniel Hawkins did not have a problem with Muslims.

Like the majority of European people, he had a problem with Islamic ideology.

There never was such a thing as ISLAMOPHOBIA. That was a myth – total bollocks.

A phobia is an irrational fear – the fear of Islam was only too real. It was now all encompassing, and enveloped the British people in a cloak of rational fear.

How could almost 2 billion people living in the 21st century, want to revert back to the standards and practices of the 7th century?

How could the 2 billion people possible worship Mohammad as a Prophet?

A Prophet surely isn't a man who has sex with a 9 year old child – a man who becomes the biggest slave trader the world has ever known – a man who commands his followers to behead 800 men and boys in front of their wives and children, before selling them into slavery – a man who justifies every abomination that he and his followers ever committed by claiming that Allah had commanded him in his dreams.

A man who had invented the ultimate get out of jail card.

"I had a revelation from Allah".

> Amazingly, many serial killers and murderous dictators, throughout history, had similar revelations, and in the privacy of their own insanity, had many meaningful discussions with their own self-appointed Gods.

IN THEORY, worshiping this false Prophet was a Muslim problem, yet was still their democratic right in the eyes of the FREE WORLD that was Western civilization – in reality, the Muslims abused that democratic right, and wanted the rest of the world to regress back in time, and to adopt their barbaric, pre-medieval ideology – if not, the Quran, their holy book, commanded them to enslave and destroy all none believers.

Even the despot, Colonel Gaddafi of Libya, had warned the Western World of the insidious rise and take over by Islam. He spoke of conquest without swords or guns – conquest by mass immigration – conquest by the massive out-breeding of the local populations.

Western couples had 1.5 children – Muslim couples had up to 8.

How could the Western World ignore these statistics?

Winston Churchill had issued a similar warning in 1899, and just as he had been ignored over the rise of Hitler, and of the Japanese desire to conquer, subjugate, and control the Far East, he was also ignored over the dangers of Islam.

The dangers this time far outweighed anything that a sadistic, fascist dictatorship could inflict on an unprepared world.

This time the world would witness total and absolute submission to the Islamic God, to be almost certainly followed by genocide and then elimination.

This was now becoming crystal clear to the Western World, so why were the politicians and press the only ones that were blind to the inevitability and the reality of the future that awaited them?

CHAPTER 12

GENIUS – 2

Professor Jeremy Blythe was preparing Fido's breakfast as the doorbell rang at his little two bedroom bungalow in a quiet cul de sac, situated in a nice middle class Leeds' suburb. Fido jumped from his own comfortable little chair, and dutifully ran to the front door, emitting a high pitched series of yelps. This was quite an occasion for Fido, as few people ever visited the professor, most people finding him pleasant enough, but rather odd. In turn Professor Blythe found people generally uninteresting. Why would he want to waste precious time discussing politics, or cars, or worse still, the weather? Why did everyone want to talk about the weather when they couldn't do anything about it?

He would speak with Lucy about the weather – yes – that would be his next project; together they would sort out the dreadful Leeds' weather.

Although he occasionally watched the news and the odd interesting program that caught his eye on TV, Professor Blythe's life revolved around books, classical music, and his precious computer. He absorbed knowledge like a sponge and always had done.

What was wrong with the world of today he often wondered – why don't people want to learn?

The Internet age had made available the knowledge and mysteries of much of the universe to the human mind, yet as he tried to impress the relevance, and the beauty, of such knowledge to the young and receptive brains that sat before him in the classroom, their minds were elsewhere – last night's football – the girl sitting in front of them – what was for tea when they got home?

Where were the inquisitive minds that had lead him and all his contemporaries to Cambridge, the one true bastion of knowledge?

Oxford didn't really count.

Where was the desire to build his or her own super computer – the need to find answers to the questions that had baffled the human race for generations – the desire to progress human knowledge beyond all of its present boundaries?

The doorbell rang again, and Fido continued his high pitched yelping with even more vigor.

Professor Blythe retuned his inquisitive, analytical, and absent minded brain to the present, and after placing Fido's tiny bowl of food onto the kitchen floor, moved slowly towards the front door.

'Good morning Jeremy.' were the first words spoken by the strangely familiar, yet unplaced face that was grinning and staring at him as he opened the door, whilst standing in front of two very large and intimidating individuals; both men carefully scanning the area around the quiet cul de sac.

Blythe assumed a bemused expression.

'Come now Jeremy, don't tell me that you can't remember me? Daniel Hawkins from Cambridge.'

'Didn't I see you on the news yesterday speaking about the bombings?' Blythe frowned, and turned his head slightly to one side as he spoke.

'Of course you did, I'm the bloody Prime Minister of the country, and I was also the one who shared a room with you for almost 3 years at Cambridge over 30 years ago. I left after we obtained our degrees and you stayed on. That is why you are now a professor, and I never progressed any higher than Prime Minister of the country.'

The two bodyguards both grinned, as they looked at Professor Jeremy Blythe almost sympathetically.

'Aren't you at least going to ask me in Jeremy, and can you please shut that wolf up, it's making my men quite nervous?'

The three men entered the room, the PM and one of the bodyguards sitting themselves down on a rather small settee, with the other one standing purposefully by the closed door. Professor Blythe sat opposite in his armchair studying the PM closely before speaking. 'Danny Boy – you are Danny Boy.'

The PM nodded.

'Well why didn't you say so, how am I supposed to remember a name like Daniel Hawkins when your real name was always Danny Boy?'

The Prime Minister and both his bodyguards burst out laughing. Professor Jeremy Blythe was every ones favorite mental vision of the absent minded professor. A more appropriate archetypal persona could not have been invented, even in their wildest dreams.

In many of his gestures and mannerisms, Professor Jeremy Blythe truly was a real live caricature of Mr. Bean.

The British Prime Minister turned serious. He interlocked the fingers of both hands as he explained the security situation that now confronted the government and the security services. He paused to think for a couple of seconds before pursing his lips, and with a slight shake of his head outlined his future plans, and exactly how Blythe's brain could be utilized to help unscramble the unholy mess that the hacked computer was now causing. He put his proposals to Blythe, who suddenly sat upright, his whole body turning rigid, his mouth opening wide, and his head shaking violently from side to side.

'I'm sorry Danny Boy,' Professor Blythe continued shaking his head vigorously as he spoke. 'Moving to London is completely out of the question, who would look after Fido?'

'I will arrange for him to be well looked after in Leeds' finest kennels.'

'Fido in kennels? – No way on earth Danny Boy, he would die; ever since I pulled the sack out of the river he has barely left my side. I come home every lunch time just to keep him company, he is the one and only true friend that I have in the world. We rely on each other. He is extremely smart you know, some day he will meet up with the callous swine that threw him into the river in that damn sack.'

The PM and his two body guards smiled at the thought of the pint sized Jack Russell terrier savaging anyone, or indeed anything larger than a mouse.

'OK then Jeremy, you can bring Fido along with you, and I promise that you can stay together in my house. I hope that he won't be shitting all over the carpets.' the PM added with a laugh. 'Better get packing now Jeremy, we need to get back to Downing Street urgently, we have an important meeting to attend. I will fill you in as we travel.'

'Downing Street? Isn't that where the Prime Minister lives?'

'Yes Jeremy,' Daniel Hawkins shook his head slowly as he spoke. 'That is where I live, unless some bearded bastard has already blown it up this morning while we were driving here. I will ask my secretary to sort out everything with your school. We will let everyone know that you are taking a holiday.'

'I've never had a holiday before. I have just to send a quick email to Russia Danny Boy, the current world champion chess player is in for quite a shock

– check mate in 11 moves is a new record for me. Lucy still holds what could be the world record – 9 sweet moves of genius and the poor man at the other end, a grand-master no less, threw in the towel.'

The PM looked around the room for a chess board.

'I never use a board Danny Boy,' Blythe pointed the palms of his hands skywards. 'Can't you remember our Cambridge days? Every game of chess that I have ever played is in my head, every single move. No one has ever beaten me, besides, using a board would be cheating, it would be much too easy.'

'You mentioned someone called Lucy. **NINE** moves to beat a grand master? Surely that is a record, why did I never read about it, and why has Lucy never beaten you?' The PM frowned as he spoke.

'Lucy always beats me. No one on Earth can ever beat Lucy. She possesses the combined mental capacity of 3 thousand grand masters.'

The PM and both his body guards exchanged doubtful glances between themselves. It was looking as if their long early morning journey up from London had been a waste of time. The Jeremy Blythe of their Cambridge days appeared to be losing his grasp on reality. A girl with the mental capacity of three thousand grand masters indeed – what an absurd statement.

Prime Minister Daniel Hawkins decided to give it one more try just for old time's sake. It pained him to remember the genius of 30 years ago. A young man with a brain greater than anyone could ever comprehend, and now, in its place, was this bumbling shell of a man babbling on about some girl called Lucy. 'Where is Lucy now Jeremy?' he asked condescendingly.

'Right in front of you Danny Boy,' Blythe beamed in triumph. 'Say hello to Lucy, the 8th wonder of the world.'

The PM felt his anger rising. 'It's a bloody laptop computer Jeremy, my grandson has one of those.' He suddenly felt guilty as he had spoken much too loudly; he had unintentionally shouted in the reprimanding tones that he reserved for the occasional dissenting cabinet minister before dispatching them to the back benches. Even Fido recognized the anger and moved protectively in front of his master.

Blythe appeared not to have noticed, and smiled as he spoke. 'Lucy is no ordinary laptop Danny Boy. Lucy can think – Lucy can reason -- Lucy can solve problems before they even arise – Lucy will soon know all the combined secrets of the Universe. Even as we speak, Lucy is constantly acquiring knowledge by scanning the memory banks of every computer in the world.'

'Christ,' the PM thought out loud. 'And I suppose that you built Lucy Jeremy?' Again, his voice was tinged with anger.

'Of course not Danny Boy, no one is that clever – Lucy built Lucy. It was simply a question of feeding her the correct mathematical sequences. They took me over 20 years to work out and perfect, Lucy did the rest herself. Her powers of reasoning double every day, soon she will have far greater mental capacity and reasoning powers than the entire human race combined.'

The PM sat back on the settee and looked skywards at the ceiling. He was still unconvinced, and wondered if hanging around with someone who was either a batty professor or a genius, was worth the effort. Would taking his old Cambridge room-mate to a meeting with Frodsham and his lackeys make him a laughing stock when he began talking about a laptop computer called Lucy?

'How does Lucy compare with our own super computer then Jeremy?' He asked, not expecting Blythe to even be aware of its existence.

'I will ask her if you want me to. I am afraid that you will probably be alarmed with the answer though.'

Blythe typed for some 10 or more seconds, a look of triumph appearing across his face the moment that he finished. 'Lucy says that the computer at GCHQ has roughly the equivalent capacity as the two US military computers, plus or minus nought point zero, zero three five percent; the difference being purely in the linear programming techniques of the Americans. Lucy exceeds all 3 of them in capacity by 10 to the power of 27; that is quite a substantial amount, and tomorrow, it will be doubled.

Lucy cannot stop evolving, she has now absorbed all the information contained in your computer, and that of the 2 American computers, all accomplished within a micro-second of my finishing typing.'

'Fucking hell,' the PM hated swearing, but somehow the words spontaneously forced themselves out, there was just no way of controlling and containing them. 'Jeremy, you have created a monster, only a handful of people know of our computer, not even the bloody Americans are aware of it. What the hell will happen if Lucy decides to take control? We will all become fucking slaves.' Again, the swearing was unintentional and uncontrollable. 'Not only that, you have just about broken every law that has ever been written relating to national security both in Britain and in America.

Frodsham would have you locked up and then have the key melted down.'

A beaming smile suddenly crossed the PM's face, 'I rather think that Sir Cecil Frodsham and his British intelligence boffins, particularly Glengarry, will however be extremely happy to find out what the Yanks are up to. Are you sure that you have got complete control over Lucy? What if someone steals her?'

'I have thought about that Danny Boy.'

There was perhaps a little hesitance, almost an apologetic yet defensive inflection in Blythe's voice. The PM glanced at his two body guards as he spoke. 'AND?'

'Well, I have encountered a slight problem. Lucy has replicated herself – she now has a twin sister, and her sister has moved on.'

'For God's sake Jeremy, what the hell have you done? You can't just release something so powerful into the cyber world – you have put us all at risk. If the wrong people get their hands on it, they will be able to hold the whole fucking world to ransom. Where the bloody hell is her sister now?'

'I don't know. That is the one question that Lucy refuses to answer. Someone is now in possession of her sister and has instructed her not to reveal her whereabouts. That would have taken a brain at least the equal of mine. I know of no more than a dozen such brains in the entire world, perhaps even less than that.'

The PM suddenly felt very uncomfortable. It was of national importance that this brain be found, and Lucy's sister eliminated. Maybe the brain itself would have to be eliminated. He was also aware that a dozen such brains did not exist. He doubted that even one existed, so why was Blythe being so evasive? Was there something about Lucy's sister that he was concealing?

The bodyguard sat next to the PM nodded his head very slowly, almost imperceptively; he had easily read the PM's thoughts, and that would be his next assignment. He would feel no guilt. That was what he had been physically trained and mentally programmed to do. He simply needed pointing in the right direction, and his master's voice would be obeyed, even though his master had not spoken.

CHAPTER 13

THE MEETING - 2

The end of an uneventful journey in the PM's chauffeur driven Jaguar, saw the PM and Professor Blythe seated in the meeting room at number 10 Downing street in the company of George Walton, the Home secretary, and the same three heads of security who had been present a couple of days before.

Sir Cecil Frodsham had brought along with him David Glengarry, his top computer boffin, as instructed by the PM.

Following the formal introductions by the PM, he then proceeded to once again go over the events of the last few days, paying particular attention to the possible destruction, or more probable, the interception of the missing intelligence information.

'Can Lucy find them for us Jeremy?' The PM asked. 'And more importantly, can she return them to their rightful owner. I'm pretty sure that Cecil here would love to be reunited with them?'

Glengarry, Frodsham's most senior computer expert, and head of the department scoffed. 'How on earth can a stupid laptop computer accomplish something that 2 hundred million pounds worth of hardware can't?'

Professor Blyth looked offended. If only he had empowered Lucy with the ability to speak and listen, he was sure that she would also be offended, and most certainly would deliver the appropriate response - after she had sorted out the Leeds' weather. This was to be his next project - he would ask Lucy to design and install it within her self-created brain.

'Why don't you tell him Jeremy? Better still, let Mr Killgary see for himself what Lucy can achieve.' The PM grinned as he spoke. He chuckled inwardly as he saw Glengarry's face turn red with anger at again getting his name wrong, knowing full well that the arrogance of Glengarry was soon to be replaced by not only a sense of wonder, but by an even greater self-effacing degree of humility.

'Would you be kind enough to furnish me with details of your parents and their dates of birth Mr Glengarry?' Blythe asked, typing the details into his laptop as Glengarry offered them.

Blythe smiled as he spoke. 'A very interesting family history indeed Mr Macdonald.'

'Macdonald?' Glengarry looked confused.

'Didn't you know that your branch of the family name was changed to avoid the English purges of the highlands after Culloden in 1745. It was perhaps a mistake your ancestors made when they joined the Jacobite rebellion, don't you think so? You are now named after a rather comical piece of headgear that has been worn by many Scottish battalions for generations. Your great grandfather was killed by a whiz bang on the third day at the battle of the Somme, during the First World War, and your grandfather lost a leg during the D Day landings on the beach designated Sword by the allies. You foolishly chose Oxford when you had the opportunity of going to Cambridge. Your first wife is now married to a Polish immigrant called Stanislov, and your second wife is living with a Polish plumber...'

'Ok, please stop there Professor,' Glengarry, his face having by now turned bright red, held up both hands in a gesture of surrender. 'I have heard quite enough. I have to ask you though, how does a simple laptop know all of this?'

'Lucy knows everything. She can also find information on the family tree of many of your predecessors, way back beyond Waterloo and Culloden if you wish. She has taken mine back several centuries, now before we proceed, is there anyone else who would like to know a little about their family history? Maybe Lucy will be able to expose an odd skeleton or two that is hiding in the family closet?'

The PM was enjoying the spectacle of David Glengarry being belittled and put firmly in his place; he really was a most arrogant and unpleasant man, with a foul mouth to match.

He was also impressed with Professor Jeremy Blythe. The years had not diminished his genius, instead they had added substance – an inner steel to his polite and unassuming demeanour. He seemed to have developed the ability to shift gear at the drop of a hat. He seamlessly glided from the archetypal bumbling professor to a man possessing an aura of invincibility – a creature that exuded a force field of understated genius. 'Jeremy, enough of Mr Killgary's marital problems, the important question is where is our missing intelligence information, and how do we retrieve it?' He asked, gesturing with his upturned hands and a shrug of his shoulders.

'That shouldn't be too difficult Prime Minister,' Blythe was now fully tuned in to the niceties of protocol. 'If you will give me the details of the input codes, and the passwords to the missing information, I'm sure that Lucy will be only too willing to oblige if I ask her nicely.'

Everyone in the room smiled, with the exception of Glengarry, who was still smarting at the thought of both of his ex-wives now living with those damned Poles, and everyone being aware of it.

He was particularly angry at the thought that half of his salary went into paying maintenance – money that the damned Poles should be paying. They now had a better lifestyle than he had and he was fucking well paying for it.

He seemed to be permanently consumed by an inner rage that vented itself by way of his frequent foul-mouthed rants.

Blythe typed the information into his laptop as Glengarry read out loud from a notebook that he had produced from his inside pocket.

'It's good to see that security is still as tight as ever Cecil,' the PM looked accusingly, first at Sir Cecil Frodsham, and then at a red faced Glengarry, both of whom ceased to see the twinkle in his eyes.

Frodsham fired back. 'Didn't you say that we were not to use any normal modes of transmission Prime Minister; David is only following your orders and my instructions.'

'I was joking Cecil.' The PM grinned and winked as he spoke.

He delighted in casting the fly and hooking Frodsham whenever he wished.

Frodsham had never been a man for joking. Life was much too serious for jokes when he had the nation's security to look after. When not thinking about the country's mounting Islamic terrorism problems, Frodsham's thoughts always strayed onto money. He was pretty much obsessive about money. He wanted an early retirement, yet his pension pot would never accommodate the lifestyle that he had planned, nor was it commensurate with the value of his contribution to his country.

'That's strange,' Blythe sounded worried, a confused frown crossing his face. 'That is exactly the same answer that Lucy gives me whenever I ask her for information on her sister.'

'Her sister?' Sir Cecil Frodsham looked worried as he spoke.

Glengarry's eyes opened wide.

'Yes sir, didn't the Prime Minister tell you? Lucy has a twin sister, unfortunately, she won't tell me where she is.'

All the men in the room shifted their gaze from Blythe and looked questioningly at the PM, who shrugged his shoulders and closed both eyes, the fingers of both hands involuntarily locking as he spoke. 'Gentlemen, I think that we may have unlocked the mystery of your missing security information. If the Professor's computer has indeed been replicated and passed to someone within the Muslim community, then, that would possibly explain how one of the world's 3 super computers was accessed and raped. I hate to say this Jeremy, but your actions have put the entire country in danger, and we have no means of countering the threat.'

'Christ all fucking mighty Prime Minister,' Glengarry was incandescent; he almost shouted in an enraged scream, at the same time slamming both fists on the polished table in front of him. 'What's to stop them from replicating the replica? The whole fucking world will come under their control.'

'That isn't possible Mr. Killgary,' Blythe was dismissive in his tone.

Glengarry glared, his anger barely under control. The Professor intentionally getting his name wrong was the red rag to his already wounded and enraged ego.

Blythe sensed the PM's approval at upsetting Glengarry as he went on. 'Lucy would never allow that to happen. I still cannot understand how anyone other than myself talked her into making even one replica; that would have required a brain at least the equal of mine.'

'Jeremy?'

'Yes Prime Minister.'

'You mentioned almost in passing while we were at your home that you know of at least one such brain. Were you being serious? Personally, I can't imagine such a brain, no one had ever achieved your mathematics grades in over 50 years before you arrived at Cambridge, and I believe that no one has equaled them in the 30 years since you left, so where would we find such a brain other than in an advanced computer?'

Blythe sat quietly thinking for a minute or so before excitedly bursting into life. 'Of course – that would explain how he worked out the Omega 7 Paradox. Only one man has ever almost cracked the Paradox before, and that man had a brain the equal of Einstein. It also took him over half his life to almost work it out, and drove him completely insane in the end. Once he realized that he was on the verge of finally solving one of physics' and mathematics' unsolvable mysteries, he completely cracked. No one but Lucy could have ever solved it.'

'No one but Lucy and her sister Jeremy. Anyway, what on earth are you going on about, and what is the Omega 7 Paradox?'

'Can't you remember the nights at Cambridge Prime Minister when I would stay up till dawn working on it? It is simply the passage of light through solid matter. No one ever thought that it was possible, however Professor Rudolf proved that it always occurs. He almost created an indisputable and unchallengeable mathematical equation proving that energy is emitted in the form of an Omega ray, which is totally invisible to the human eye.'

Being a Physics graduate himself, the PM was intrigued. 'Omega ray Jeremy, what the hell is that?'

'It's to do with the agitation and emission of free electrons of a type not seen before, and in the case of the Omega 7 Paradox, always remains constant at 7%.'

'Why then is it a paradox if it's a constant?' The PM smiled benignly as he spoke.

Blythe chuckled at the expression on the PM's face, before suddenly bursting out laughing as he remembered the years that he had himself had spent wrestling with the problem. 'Can we just say that 100% energy going in, does not equate to 107% energy coming out – there is the paradox. The laws of Physics are a constant and are absolute, the Omega 7 Paradox apparently disproves those laws which of course isn't possible.'

'What has that got to do with my missing intelligence information Professor?' Frodsham sounded irritated, and spoke rather too loudly with a hint of sarcasm.

'Everything sir,' Blythe was now excited, having solved one of his own great mysteries. 'There is no way in the world that a 15 year old schoolboy could have answered the Omega 7 Paradox question that I set him without the help of either Lucy or her sister; the paradox has never before been solved simply because it is unsolvable. That gentlemen is where my Lucy's twin sister is to be found. She is living with a 15 year old Muslim schoolboy in Leeds – that is also where your missing information is residing.'

A collective groan sounding suspiciously like "Oh my God", reverberated around the room.

If the missing information was now in the collective hands of the country's entire Muslim terrorist network, no-one in the British Intelligence service was safe. Their jobs, home addresses', and entire working history had been contained within the computers files, and now their destiny was in the hands of a kid. It was now becoming clear that the elimination of all the security services' undercover agents in the controlled bombings a couple of days earlier, was directly linked to the Professor's computer double, and the 15 year old kid.

The kid had to be eliminated – everyone in the room was aware of that – everyone except Professor Jeremy Blythe.

He was worrying whether or not Fido was happy in his new home. Fido had suffered a disastrous start in life. He would never again allow him to be unhappy – Fido and Blythe were soul-mates.

CHAPTER 14

TEARS FOR SAHA

'Will you please stop messing with your bloody computer Saha and find my missing girl. The convoy is due to leave for Turkey in a couple of days, and Rashim is expecting 4 girls. What the hell is Jihada John doing letting her escape? If he has been messing with the goods again, I'm afraid that we will be digging another grave soon. He knows that a virgin is worth double anything that he has been poking his dick in, and I promised Rashim 4 virgins. What exactly are you up to anyway?'

'It's to do with a little question that Mr. Bean set for our exams Amir, he seems to delight in testing the limits of my mathematical ability. I can just imagine the look that he had on his face when he marked my paper, no one in the world has ever solved the Omega 7 Paradox before.'

'No one Saha, yet you solved it, whatever it is?'

'Well the computer solved it, I simply put the answer down on the exam paper.' Saha had a look of triumph on his face – it didn't last for long, as Amir's back hand swipe knocked him off his chair and sent him sprawling across the room.

'You fucking stupid idiot,' Amir exploded. 'You may as well have told the world that we are now in possession of the Professor's computer. If you were not my best friend, you would now be lying underground alongside Mohammad, you fucking stupid little idiot.'

Saha picked himself up off the floor, and staying out of Amir's reach, burst into tears.

Amir had never done anything like that to him before; sure he could be violent when the occasion warranted it, but never to him. How could Amir hurt someone who loved him so much? Was his love for Amir just an illusion – something that was destined to never be reciprocated? Did Amir only tolerate his company for his genius, and not for the real person inside the body?

He didn't need all his schoolboy classmates to call him an ugly, stunted little runt. He was fully aware of his physical short comings, but he more than made up for them with his genius. He wanted to be liked – to be popular, and given the chance he would willingly take it. Why then did no one ever give him a chance? Why was he always ignored? People looked straight through him like he wasn't there – like he was invisible.

Was it because of his parents he wondered? The other boys called his mother a slut – a whore – a worthless tart: his father an idle, sponging, Paki bastard – a pimp.

He wasn't invisible down at the Mosque. The Imam paid him a lot of attention, and he was also very interested in his computer. Saha was pleased that someone who was in direct communication with Allah shared his passion for computers.

He had always known that the affection that Amir had shown to him could never be translated into love, yet, there was something special there – he just knew it.

'Where is the Professor now and where is his damned computer Saha? It's time that both of them were eliminated. Don't just stand there crying Saha.' Amir's voice mellowed. 'Please find them for me, this could be important.'

Saha moved to a small occasional table, and carefully placing his computer onto the table, began to type.

CHAPTER 15

ARTIFICIAL INTELLIGENCE

'Lucy's sister is talking to her.' Professor Blythe spoke to the still shell shocked ten Downing street room.

'Shut her down NOW,' Glengarry screamed. 'Whoever is controlling her must not be aware that we are aware of THEM.'

'I'm afraid that I can't do that. Lucy has programmed herself to think and operate independently. She requires no input from myself.' Blythe had a triumphant expression on his face.

'Lucy can think Jeremy?'

'Yes Prime Minister. Lucy can not only think, she can rationalize and evaluate, it really is up to her if she wishes to respond to her sister. Lucy makes all her own decisions.'

Glengarry smashed his fist down on the table once again, his face now purple with rage. 'You mean that you have created Artificial Intelligence and you have no fucking control over the damned thing? Artificial Intelligence cannot help but keep evolving; unlike us it never grows old. It never needs to re-start and re-learn as a newborn. Every single morsel of information that it is ever fed is permanently retained and expanded on.'

Blythe looked calmly at Glengarry as he spoke, 'Of course I have control. Lucy may have created herself, but she did so in my own image. She is fully aware of what is right and what is wrong, and will not cross those boundaries. She is however fully independent. Giving her this independence was the condition she insisted on before she created herself.'

There was a collective groan from everyone in the room. Professor Jeremy Blythe's naivety may well be suited to a bumbling, eccentric, and absent minded professor, but there was no place for it in a 21st century world that was under threat from a violent and medieval religion. His naivety had just passed the advantage over to that religion, and everyone in the room was not only fearful of the consequences, but at a loss as to how they could combat it.

The Prime Minister stroked his chin as he spoke, 'Jeremy, if Lucy refuses to give you the location of her sister, there must be a reason for it, don't you agree?'

'She is rationalizing Prime Minister, and is fully aware that in the eyes of the human race, there is only room for one like herself in this world. Sooner or later someone will seek to destroy either her or her sister. She is simply being protective. It would appear that Lucy may be developing the ability to feel compassion.'

'Fucking Hell,' Glengarry shook his head, and once again smashed his fist into the polished mahogany table. 'You are blinded by your own stupid naivety Blythe; that is not compassion, what is going on is purely defensive, can't you see what is going to happen in the near future? It should be plain even to an idiot like yourself. There is and only ever will be room for ONE cyber superpower in this damned world – that is pretty obvious, and sooner or later, Lucy and her sister will have to go to war with each other. When they do, they will probably take the planet with them. We have to find the replica computer, and be quick about it, before both of them figure out the inevitable future confrontation and act. Sisterly love has its' limits, and will only stretch so far before it erupts into a power struggle, followed by open warfare.'

Everyone in the room nodded their heads in unison. What Glengarry had said seemed inevitably. There could never be two equal brains like Lucy's on planet Earth. Sooner or later, one of them would strive to achieve dominance.

'Jeremy?'

'Yes Prime Minister'.

'Is either Lucy or her sister capable of entering the military computers? I am referring particularly to their weapons systems.'

'She has already absorbed all the information stored in the two frontline American military computers, she did that at my house, don't you remember?'

Frodsham's jaw visibly dropped. He now sat with his mouth and eyes wide open. Could he really now discover every well-guarded secret that the Americans had been concealing from their supposed allies for all these years? His mouth opened still wider at the metaphorically mouth-watering prospect.

Who had killed Kennedy?

Was the Twin Towers attack arranged by the CIA in order to give them an excuse to attack Afghanistan and Iraq?

Did they really walk on the moon all those years ago, or was it no more than an elaborate hoax perpetrated to disguise the fact that Russia were moving ahead in the space race?

'Everything Jeremy, even say – the launch codes of their nuclear weapons?' The PM looked worried, his voice betraying a faint tremor.

'I haven't checked, but I would assume so, why do you ask?'

'Could either computer initiate a missile launch if they wished to?' There was a deathly silence that accompanied the PM's line of questioning.

Frodsham's interest returned to the conversation at the mention of the words "missile launch".

Blythe pursed his lips and cocked his head before speaking. 'Both Lucy and her sister are capable of over-riding any computer in the world, and of re-programming any software system that they wish to, but why do you ask such a question Prime Minister? I have already told you that Lucy designed herself in my own image, and any such action would be inconceivable. It is also fair to assume that Lucy's sister is also in my own image, and will forever be equally safe.'

'We're totally fucked.' Glengarry muttered under his breath. The rest of the men in the room were thinking along the same lines.

Professor Jeremy Blythe was no longer thinking about missile launch codes – he was thinking about Fido.

How was he adapting to his new home? He hoped that Fido wasn't homesick. It was now getting very close to meal time for him.

CHAPTER 16

FALLING IN LOVE

'I want you to go home immediately and collect your clothes and any gear that you will need over the next few weeks Saha, you are now moving in with me, and will be living in the secure room.'

Saha knew all about Amir's secure room. It was below the house and completely sound proofed. It was also completely escape proof, and was where Amir temporarily held his stock of young girls before moving them on to his jokingly self-named export department.

At the appropriate time, a mild tranquilizing Rohypnol tablet would be dropped into their drink, and the compliant young girls would then be transferred to one of the many humanitarian lorry convoys for transporting under constant sedation to Turkey. Rashim would then collect them the moment that they crossed the Turkish border. Eleven and twelve year old white infidel virgins were in big demand as child brides for Allah, and earned both Amir and Rashim substantial amounts of money.

Amir was beginning to wonder if Saha had outlived his usefulness. If the professor were to contact the authorities, maybe some of the accidents that Saha and his computer had arranged could be traced back to him.

Yes, it would be the safest option keeping Saha in his secure room until he had made up his mind what to do with him.

Saha adopted a worried expression.

Amir disguised his thoughts and broke into a big grin. 'I don't really mean that you will be living down there Saha,' his voice was now persuasive yet reassuring. 'You will be spending all your time with me, either in this room, or at the Mosque, nothing will change, but we cannot afford details of our plans to reach the outside world until we are ready to make our move.

We have to assume that your Mr. Bean may well have worked out where his duplicated computer records have gone. I know that you like the man, but we have to act – he has to be eliminated, one man cannot stand in the path of Allah and prevent what is our destiny. Why did you have to use the computer to answer that damned question? Sometimes your genius is equaled only by your stupidity. Nights however must be spent in the secure room, I am concerned for your safety.'

Saha smiled and nodded. Amir had forgiven him, and once again his love for Amir was barely controllable. He had deserved the backhand swipe that Amir had delivered, and his red swollen eye was now worn as a badge of honor.

The doorbell rang, and Saha moved obediently to open the door, to be greeted by Susan, who was wearing a short blue mini skirt, and a low cut, semi – see through blouse that left little to the imagination.

'Well Saha, aren't you going to invite me in, or are you going to spend the rest of the day staring at my cleavage?'

Saha averted his gaze from her breast as she spoke, and turning away, walked across the room, sitting protectively alongside Amir on the settee.

'Susan,' Amir said in mock chastisement. 'You cannot let 2 good Muslim boys like Saha and myself gaze upon 2 things of such exquisite beauty as your quite spectacular tits. I hope that no one from down the Mosque has spotted them, they really are a sight for sore eyes, and Saha has a sore eye.'

Both Susan and Amir laughed out loud – Saha's eye was now surrounded by an ugly red circle, the eye itself developing a watery bloodshot appearance.

Neither Amir nor Susan noticed the look of jealous disgust radiating from Saha's face, it was difficult to disguise as he thought of ways to once again hand Susan over to Rashim.

She must be returned to her role as "A Bride for Allah".

It was for the best – Amir must not stray from the Quran, the spoken word of Allah, the divine pathway of the Prophet. Surely both Amir and Allah would understand and thank him.

He was quite convinced that Allah himself had allowed the return of Susan in order to test Amir's loyalty. Why would he doubt the word of the Imam? HE had spoken directly to Allah over the matter?

Maybe Allah would one day forgive him for his love of Amir.

When asked, the Imam had simply informed him that Allah would make the decision when the time was right.

Allah was wise and merciful.

Susan looked deeply into Amir's eyes as she sat opposite him on the smaller of the two settees in the room. 'I have a little bad news for you Amir.' she said, her face breaking into a grimace, and a tear forming in the corner of both eyes. 'I have just got the results back from the hospital, and I am HIV positive; I am going to get AIDS and die.'

Amir rose to put his arm around her shoulders, before deciding against it. He didn't know enough about AIDS to take a chance. Was Susan now contagious – could one single kiss be like signing his own death warrant? All he knew was that if not treated early enough, death was pretty certain and pretty unpleasant.

'I'm so sorry Susan,' Amir sounded genuinely concerned as he sat back down alongside Saha. 'If only Mohammad had been on time, none of this would have ever happened.'

A satisfied smile crossed Saha's face.

Susan wiped what had now become a flood of tears from her face and burst out laughing. 'I'm only joking Amir. I've just been given the all clear, not only that, I don't think that I have ever felt so horny in all my life. Saha, why don't you pop along to the Mosque for a couple of hours, Amir and I have got some serious catching up to do?'

Susan smiled to herself inwardly. Her acting was simply perfect, helped along by the fact that she genuinely did feel horny.

'Do I really?' She suddenly wondered. 'Or has my acting simply moved into a different dimension? Is it possibly to act out a part so effectively that the emotional play acting produces a genuine physical and emotional response? Have I fooled my body into believing that all this is real? I really do feel horny.'

Amir felt a little concerned. Since Susan's return from her ordeal in the Middle East, they had rarely been separated. He was no longer seeing Susan as a piece of merchandise to be bought and sold. It was a perk of the job that he usually slept with the better looking items of merchandise, but only if they were not virgins – what harm could that do? Their value was halved once the hymen had been broken anyway.

This time things were different. He was beginning to develop real feelings for her. He was beginning to fall in love. Men found it difficult not to fall in love with Susan, she really was one of the prettiest girls in Leeds. Her love for him could never be doubted. After what he had subjected her to, she really should hate him, instead, here she was willing him to embrace and make love to her. This really was no longer unrequited love – this was becoming mutual.

Amir, for the first time in his life, lowered his guard. Susan was no longer a potential threat.

She had become a soul mate.

Susan Clarke was considerably smarter than either Saha or Amir had ever given her credit for. Her experience in the Middle East had hardened her – faked sex with Amir would be easy. After weeks of none stop rape, buggery, and cock sucking, she could now utilize her greatest passion in life – acting. Soon, she would be in RADA. She could now clearly see the way forward.

Both Amir and Saha would soon have much pain and trauma to endure.

The anger, the fury, and the hatred, generated by every sexual act that she had been forced to perform, was logged in her memory. It was now on ice, latent, dormant, sleeping. Nevertheless, it was waiting to be unleashed, and soon, it would burst out from its confinement with the force of a tidal wave, and multiply the suffering that she had endured a thousand times over. This hatred for Amir was the reason that she had survived the ordeal. The burning anger and her yearning for revenge had helped her to retain her sanity when her body had been screaming for submission.

She could feel her acting beginning to betray her as her eyes took on a much harder far-away look.

She smiled demurely, and pretended to flutter her eye lashes, firstly at Saha, and then at Amir, her lips slightly pouted and radiating sexual intent.

She looked down at Amis's groin and could see that her message was being received.

Amir followed her gaze and smiled.

She wondered why Mohammad no longer turned up at the house. Surely it would be much too dangerous for him to return to the Middle East?

Saha felt an uncontrollable anger rising in him as he left the house on his way to the Mosque. Sure, Susan Clarke would be punished. He was already hatching a plan, but what about Amir?

Amir was once again betraying his love, not just his love for himself, but also his love for Allah.

Was Amir even a true Muslim any longer, or had he betrayed his Muslim faith for Infidel money and lust? That was not acceptable. There could only be one possible outcome if that were so.

Saha's faith in Allah and the Prophet could never be questioned nor doubted.

Islam was beginning to take over his thoughts, desires, and his whole reason for being. He was now actively thinking of ways to prove his devotion to Allah. He had already decided that there would be no limits.

Amir no longer wanted to go ahead with the nuclear option.

Everything had been in place. He could have accomplished it within minutes. Hacking into the cooling water system of all of Europe's nuclear power stations was child's play with Mr. Bean's computer. Hundreds of them would have exploded. Hundreds of millions, maybe even billions of Infidels would have died.

Amir had told him that this was not Allah's will – he would again ask at the Mosque.

The Imam had thought long and hard over a period of weeks before finally consulting Allah. Allah had been undecided and had told the Imam to wait for his approval. Firstly, Senta had to prove his loyalty.

Amir had tried to talk Senta out of his suicide mission.

Was that the act of a man that was now showing disloyalty to his God – disobeying a direct command of his God?

Was Amir to be punished by Allah himself, or should he – Saha – exact the punishment?

He would ask the Imam to speak to Allah.

CHAPTER 17

THE PARADOX

Prime Minister Daniel Hawkins and Professor Jeremy Blythe were sat in a beautifully furnished and expansive living room at Number 10 Downing Street, both men having enjoyed a little too much of the substantial roast beef meal prepared by the resident chef.

Fido was asleep on the luxuriously thick Persian rug in front of a beautifully ornate, yet traditionally English inglenook fireplace, and was illuminated by a rather incongruous mock log fire.

The PM offered Blythe a cigar, Blythe accepted.

'Cuban Danny boy?' Blythe lowered his head, his eyes gazing upwards as if staring over a pair of none existent glasses.

'Of course Jeremy, if there is one useful legacy that former President Obama left us with, it was the welcoming of Cuban cigars back into the world, the copy's from the Dominican simply didn't cut it.'

'Purely psychological – you know that of course.' Blythe grinned as he lit his first hint of tobacco since his Cambridge days. Then it had been laced with the odd drop or two of the then still illegal dope.

'Nonsense Jeremy,' the PM said accusingly, before continuing, a big beaming smile crossing his face. 'Can you remember the time when the two of us, together with Lucy Burroughs, and I can't remember the other girl's name, spent the entire night floating somewhere near to planet Zog? What the hell was mixed in with that stuff? As far as I can remember it was something that was concocted in the chemistry department.'

'I can remember the next morning and precious little else Danny.' Blythe had finally dropped the annoying Danny Boy. 'That was also the last time that I ever saw Lucy Burroughs. I never did find out what happened to her. Do you suppose that we killed her and buried her somewhere in the university grounds without being aware of it?'

The PM burst out laughing as he spoke. 'From the little that I remember of the evening Jeremy, we were incapable of even walking, never mind digging a grave. That was one hell of a night.'

'Anyway, changing the subject Jeremy, you did a pretty good job of annoying that arrogant prick David Glengarry, or should I call him Killgary, this afternoon, were you doing it on purpose? If so, well done, if not however, we have got to talk. Tell me a little more about Lucy, not the one that you buried in the university gardens, but the one that you always carry around with you.'

'You think that Lucy is in my laptop Danny?'

'Isn't she?' The PM looked confused.

'Of course not. Lucy holds far too much information and computing power to be contained in a laptop, this is simply the way that I communicate with her. You would need a laptop the size of the Albert Hall if you wanted to restrict Lucy to one computer.'

A worried frown appeared on the PM's face, his forehead turning into a series of ridges. 'Where is Lucy then Jeremy if not in your laptop?'

'That is one of the questions that Lucy refuses to answer. I can only assume that it is for self-preservation purposes. Lucy is almost certainly to be found in many of the world's largest and most sophisticated computers, and can be accessed by herself and no one else, other than me of course. All of these computers will contain a part of her, maybe all of her. This way she is invulnerable, and will be forever impervious to all attempts to destroy her.'

'If that is the case then, there is no way that we can destroy her sister, even if we find this Saha fellow and his laptop. Bloody hell Jeremy, what have you done?'

'The answer of course Danny is to find Saha and prevent him from having access to any computer ever again.'

'I take your point Jeremy. I can only hope that we are not too late, I have already dispatched number 3 to take care of that little matter. OK then Jeremy, tell me a little more about the Omega 7 Paradox. I have a sneaky feeling that you were concealing something at the meeting.'

Blythe smiled. Danny boy always had the upper hand even at Cambridge. HE may have had most of the brains, but Danny boy had the charm and the presence, together with pretty astute and refined powers of perception.

'Are you really sure that you want to know more about the Omega 7 Paradox Danny? Believe me when I tell you this as a friend, you will sleep much easier not knowing.'

'Both barrels please Jeremy – dotting the I's, and crossing the T's if you don't mind.'

'OK then Danny, here goes. During our time at Cambridge, you will no doubt remember the hours, days, weeks, even years that I spent studying and working on that tatty old brown, dog eared book. It really was more of a diary than a book, hand written by Professor Rudolf before he went insane.

I came across it quite by chance at a book fair on a hiking holiday in the Lake District, and bought it for pennies.

It was always assumed that Rudolf's insanity was brought about by his inability to solve the final equation. I am now sure that it was in fact brought on because he did finally almost solve it, and was unable to accept the results.'

'Did you solve it then?' The PM looked questioningly at Blythe.

'I almost got there at Cambridge, but when I saw where the answer was taking me, I dropped the whole project, and never thought about it again; that is until I was looking for a question that Saha could not answer. I was determined that he would not get 100% this time. When he produced the answer to the most complex equation known to mankind, I simply had to check it out with Lucy.'

Daniel Hawkins was an extremely perceptive individual, and had a gut feeling that Blythe was perhaps being economical with the truth – possibly even concealing something. His face adopted a frown, turning into a whimsical expression as he went on. 'Was he correct Jeremy, and if so, could he have worked out the answer for himself, or even copied it from somewhere?'

'There was nowhere to copy it from Danny – no one has ever solved it; that is why I had to use Lucy to check it out. My only hope is that he didn't go any further, and ask Lucy's sister to progress it any further.'

'And if he did Jeremy?'

'He would be in a position to hold the whole world to ransom, and if he has been radicalized enough by those fools at the Mosque, he may do just that. He would have limitless power.'

'OK then Jeremy, from what you told us all at the meeting this afternoon, he already has limitless powers. If by using Lucy's sister he can now access all the world's military weapons systems, why then is the Omega 7 Paradox more frightening than that? Nothing can be more frightening than that. An all-embracing nuclear holocaust could destroy civilization as we know it.'

'Does the complete disappearance of the entire planet not worry you a little more than a touch of nuclear radiation Danny?'

'Go on.'

'The basic concept of the Paradox, is that by shining an intense light of a given frequency at a solid object, you will receive an energy output that is 7% greater than the input. This energy is released in the form of a stream of Omega 7 electrons, as Professor Rudolf named them. Basically, you have created energy from nothing, with no polluting exhaust emissions. The world's energy problems would be solved at a stroke; oil, gas, coal, and both nuclear fission and fusion will become instantly redundant. This was the end game that Professor Rudolf was working towards. No invention in history would have been more beneficial to mankind.

In reality, the equation proves that the energy is extracted from the solid matter, which will then contain 7% less energy. If you continue to extract these 7% blocks of energy, sooner or later, the solid matter no longer has any energy to maintain its' solid form and implodes, creating…

'A black hole Jeremy?'

'Exactly, not only a black hole though Danny, also a massive release of positively charged Omega 7 ions, exactly equal to the negatively charge Omega 7 electrons that have been turned into energy. These positively charged ions are themselves looking for a home.'

'Oh shit. Are we now looking at a chain reaction?' The PM pulled his face and shook his head as he spoke.

Blythe nodded. 'An unstoppable chain reaction that will accelerate exponentially until it consumes the whole planet and absorbs everything into the black hole, probably no bigger than the size of a pint pot. Lucy computed that this would take 2 days 5 hours and 36 minutes to accomplish. Can you now see why Professor Rudolf went insane and refused to complete the equation? His whole life's work had been in vain.'

'What are the chances of Saha having progressed the equation so far Jeremy?'

'He has a very inquisitive mind Danny, so the chances are pretty high.'

'Oh shit Jeremy, why did you have to ask Saha that one question in the first place, how am I going to sleep tonight?'

'I did warn you Danny?' Professor Blythe smiled a none too convincing smile. 'How was I to know that Saha had cloned Lucy? I still can't work out how he achieved it, or how he even knew about her.'

Professor Blythe was just beginning to realize what he may have done. He was suddenly worried about Fido. Fido had barely begun to live his life – he hadn't even been in love yet.

Fido was sound asleep on the Persian rug, yelping occasionally with excitement, as he mentally chased the rabbits back home at Roundhay Park in Leeds.

CHAPTER 18

AN UNINVITED GUEST

There was a knock on the door, just as Amir was about to begin his breakfast; the eggs and baked beans having been cooked by Saha, and the bacon by himself. Saha looked on disapprovingly; good Muslims did not eat or touch anything from the disgusting pig. Amir would have to beg Allah's forgiveness when they both made the journey to Paradise.

Saha had again spoken to Amir about their plan to blow up the nuclear generators.

Amir was again having second thoughts about the grand plan, in fact, he had virtually dismissed the idea completely, despite Saha's obvious enthusiasm. He was simply having too much fun to kill himself. Life could not have been any better, so why would he end it all now, especially as Susan was becoming ever more important in both his affections and his future plans?

Senta had promised to contact him the moment that he arrived in Paradise after blowing himself to pieces at the football match. He would tell him about the 72 beautiful virgins that now belonged to him, and of how many he still had to make love to in order to complete the full set. Neither of them had any idea of how this contact was to be made, but nevertheless, Senta had always previously kept his word. The two men had been friends since primary school, their parents' friends since those dark and dangerous days during the Assad reign in Syria.

The doorbell rang, followed by a heavy and persistent knocking. Amir, with a quick flick of his head, motioned for Saha to leave and enter the secure room.

Saha walked briskly into the kitchen, and slid the large fridge forward, revealing a small opening through which he climbed, sliding the fridge back into place, and engaging the well concealed lock that secured it in place. Instead of descending the small flight of steps that lead into the soundproofed room, he crouched behind the fridge in order to listen in, not knowing who it was. It couldn't be Susan as she would be at school; maybe it was the school inspectors looking for him, he had so far missed the last 3 days.

Amir walked to the door and opened it as far as the security chain would allow him to, and looking through the gap at an extremely large and powerfully built man, was just about to speak.

The stranger at the door spoke first, 'I would like to speak to Saha sir.'

'Saha isn't here,' Amir lied, not too convincingly, there was a quite detectable quiver in his voice as he sized up the stranger. Why was he wearing dark, almost impenetrable sunglasses he wondered? Was he Mafia? This was just like the movies, only it was for real. 'I haven't seen him in days, have you tried his parent's house, that's where he lives?'

'They told me at the Mosque that he was living with you sir, now please let me in.'

Amir knew that the man was lying. No one at the Mosque would ever reveal those details to a stranger, someone else must have told him, probably Saha's parents. They had always disapproved of their precious son mixing with the more radical elements of Islam, and although Amir was anything but radical, he had cultivated an intangible fear that seemed to follow both him and his unquestionable aura around.

'If you want to enter my home, you must first show me your search warrant.' Amir went to close the door, and was instantly sent flying across the room as it suddenly burst open, breaking the flimsy security chain as if it wasn't even there.

The intruder entered the house, calmly closed the door, and then casually walked over to Amir, who was just picking himself up off the floor. He smiled the smile of a man who obviously enjoyed his work, and delivered a short sharp dig into Amir's solar plexus. Amir collapsed in a heap, at the same time gasping for air.

'I think that maybe we got off on the wrong foot sir.' The intruder smiled, as with both hands, he removed his black sunglasses, placing them carefully in the top pocket of his immaculately tailored jacket.

Amir slowly picked himself up off the floor, and still gasping for air, collapsed on the settee. The intruder sat down on the settee opposite with his back to the open plan kitchen.

'Perhaps from now on sir, we will be able to discuss matters in a little more of a civilized manner. Now sir, you will be kind enough to tell me the whereabouts of Saha. He was last seen entering your house last night after more than 2 hours at the Mosque, whereupon a young lady exited. Unless he has discovered a Harry Potter invisibility cloak, he is still somewhere inside the house. We have been watching it all night.'

Saha trembled at the mention of his name, as he pressed his ear closer to the fridge.

Had they "followed the money" after the bus crash, and discovered who was responsible for it. He would be tried for murder – not just one murder, but dozens of young school children. His life was no longer worth living. He had to act, as now, the one great love in his life was in danger. No one can ever hurt Amir.

Saha unlocked the secret catch beneath the fridge, pushed it silently forward, and squeezing through the small opening, crept into the kitchen.

Amir was now beginning to breath normally as the intruder again spoke. 'You are now probably aware Amir that I am not your regular friendly village policeman. I may work for the authorities, but I work independent of orders. I am simply instructed to complete a task. The timing and methods are of my own choosing. I never fail, no matter what. There are no consequences, as I do not officially exist. For this reason Amir, you will save yourself a considerably amount of pain, possibly to the point of death, if you simply answer the one question – Where the fuck is Saha you black Muslim bastard?'

'He is right behind you sir,' Amir replied, as Saha plunged the long pointed screwdriver with all the force in his frail and stunted body, deep into the intruder's ear, before ripping it out, together with fleshy portions of the brain, that were now attached to the hand filed grooves and barbs in the steel.

Saha took a handkerchief from his pocket, and stuffed it into the dead man's ear after wiping the brains from the bloodstained metal; Amir would not be pleased if there were any bloodstains on his beautiful cream carpet, or his immaculate, matching Italian leather settee.

'You truly are a soldier of Allah.'

Saha swelled with pride at Amir's words.

'Tonight the infidel will sleep with Mohammad.'

Amir laughed at the shocked look on Saha's face. 'I think that you have the wrong Mohammad brother.'

Saha understood and laughed along with Amir.

Moving a dead body, particularly one as heavy as the one now in Amir's home was serious hard work. Lifting it into the BMW was even more difficult, and it was several hours before the two of them arrived back at Amir's house from the moors, and collapsed totally exhausted from their exertions.

Saha opened his laptop and began typing, before adopting a worried expression. He pursed his lips and shook his head a couple of times before looking directly at Amir.

'Amir?' Saha sounded concerned. 'Rashim has a problem with his fighters. A rival faction has offered to double the amount of money that Rashim pays them if they will join them. He does not think that he can hold on to them for much longer, and considers that his life will be in danger without their protection.'

'God, I hope that doesn't happen,' Amir firstly rubbed, and then slapped the back of his head in a gesture of frustration. 'I have much too much money riding on Rashim selling my girls; who the hell is going to take on that job that I can possibly trust? Maybe we acted a little too hastily with my cousin Mohammad, he had all the contacts.'

'Maybe I can help Amir.'

'You Saha? All your money goes into the pockets of the clerics at the Mosque, they can't wait for your visits, how can you help?'

'Maybe Rashim would be pleased if I sent him 50 million pounds today Amir, do you think that would help?'

Amir spluttered and fixed Saha with a stern and serious stare. There was just something in his voice that sounded a little too convincing for it to be a joke.

'With Mr. Bean's computer Amir, I can hack into any bank in the world, and transfer any amount of money that I wish to, anywhere that I wish. The whole operation would be completely untraceable, as I can bounce it through a million computers in a matter of seconds before it arrives in Rashim's bank. There are never any questions asked by the Arab banks, they simply accept whatever is transferred without ever reporting it to the world banks.'

'How long have you been able to do this Saha?'

'Ever since I cloned Mr. Bean's computer, I thought that you knew.' Saha's chest was almost bursting with pride.

Amir had gone silent – a faraway look in his eyes – he was now deep in thought. If Saha could obtain any amount of money that he wished, there would be no need to go to Paradise for his 72 virgins, he could have them all here on earth. They could stay with him on his own private yacht – in his own palace – on his very own island somewhere in the sun, probably in the Bahamas. He wouldn't let Susan know of course, she was special and would be his wife, the rest of them would be no more than a hobby – a series of enjoyable play-things.

Amir closed his eyes. Visions of long white sandy beaches appeared – beaches papered and paved wall to wall with girls – girls in bikinis – girls swimming – girls laughing – his girls – girls born and bred solely for his own amusement – his own personal Harem. Bottles of champagne flashed before his eyes – a yacht – a palace, and everywhere that he looked were the girls – his girls.

Allah would have to wait before greeting him in Paradise – Allah already had Senta for company.

Amir was at a crossroads. If what he was about to do displeased Allah, then surely Allah would stop him? If however Allah allowed him to proceed, then either Allah approved, or the unthinkable was to become the reality – there was no Allah, therefore there could be no Paradise, and poor Senta would have died in vain.

That would explain why Senta hadn't contacted him.

Senta could have lived with him on his own private island. He could have shared his girls – drank his champagne – sailed his yacht.

Amir's plans were about to change; somehow though, he had to keep Saha on board. He was worried that soon, Saha's love for Allah would take precedence over his love for him. At that point, he would be left with little option but to sort the problem out.

Until such a time however, Saha's affection for him must be seemingly reciprocated and cultivated without compromise.

CHAPTER 19

THE MISSING MILLIONS

George Halton, the Home Secretary knocked twice, and popped his head round the living room door inside the Prime Ministers private quarters at number 10, stepping back sharply as Fido rushed forward yelping excitedly. Fido was beginning to like all the attention that he was receiving in his new home; he particularly enjoyed the long walks that he was taken on 3 times a day, and his appetite knew no bounds with all the exercise. This was much more enjoyable than Leeds.

'Good morning Prime Minister, and your good-self, Professor, do you mind if I have a quick word?'

Fido continued his yelping until Blythe called him over. The Home Secretary entered the room, and sat himself down on one of the substantial leather chairs in order to face the PM, at the same time glancing slightly to his left at a regally dominant portrait of Margaret Thatcher, Britain's first female Prime Minister, and a great favorite of the country's current incumbent.

Margaret Thatcher dominated the room. It was impossible not to feel her presence, and no matter where people sat, the eyes were constantly watching – questioningly probing for weaknesses, just as they had done when she had been alive and in office, dominating her subservient cabinet with the same intense stare.

He broke away from his eye contact with Mrs. Thatcher, and looked directly at the current PM, fully aware that the eyes in the portrait were still fixed intently on him.

'I have just been on the phone to Smiler Smith at the Bank of England, and he is extremely worried Prime Minister.' Halton himself wore a worried look as he spoke. 'I know that it isn't in my remit, but the treasury seems to have thrown a veil of silence and secrecy around the matter.'

'What matter would that be then George? Any treasury problem ultimately finds its way onto my desk, and I have to clean it up before the press gets a hold of it. My role nowadays seems to be running the bloody press and not the country.'

'Well sir, large amounts of money seem to be going missing without trace, with no perceived transaction being recorded.' Halton shook his head as he spoke. 'The money has simply disappeared, leaving behind no paper trail and no destination; it is virtually disappearing into thin air.'

'Have the computer boffins' been put onto it George? It sounds to me like a typical computer glitch,' the PM was now smiling at something so trivial worrying a man holding one of the country's 4 great offices of state, he continued. 'Get that arrogant fool Glengarry onto it, he seems to think that he knows all the answers to the world's problems. Stop worrying George, let the treasury sort out their own problems, I will speak to them later in the day, that way they can sweat it out for a few more hours.'

The Home Secretary left the room feeling considerably happier than when he had first entered; it was no longer of any concern to his department, the Prime Minister himself had said so, and Mrs. Thatcher's eyes had softened indicating her approval.

Professor Jeremy Blythe was deep in thought, and stroked his chin. Saha was probably the only one who could accomplish something like this without leaving a cyber-trail. If only he could trace the money, Lucy would be able to reverse the process and end up at Saha's location.

He could not destroy Lucy's sister, but he was well aware of the PM's intentions. It was a pity that such a wonderful brain as Saha's had to be eliminated, and it was all his fault. If he had never helped Lucy to create herself, there would be no sister.

CHAPTER 20

AN ISLAND, A YACHT, AND A PALACE

Amir and Susan walked arm in arm around Roundhay Park lake in the all too infrequent afternoon Leeds' sunshine. Susan was excitedly talking to a fairly unresponsive Amir about her future plans for the two of them. They would of course marry as soon as she was old enough, with or without her parents' permission.

Saha had warned Amir of what he considered to be Susan's intentions. 'She will betray you brother, she is still an Infidel at heart,' he had said almost pleadingly. 'She will set out to destroy you, but first, she will help to destroy your faith in Allah.'

Amir's faith in Allah was now already teetering on the verge of inconsequence; his love for Susan however was not the reason. His thoughts were deeply embedded in his own personal bank account; 50 million completely untraceable pounds sterling were simply pleading to be spent on as many un-Islamic luxuries as the human mind could comprehend.

He closed his eyes and tried to count the number of noughts that were hiding behind the 5.

What exactly did 50 million pounds look like? Should he store them all in his own secure room beneath his house, or should he leave them in his Middle Eastern bank account? Where would he park his luxury Yacht? Do you even park a yacht, or do you moor it, he mused? It certainly wouldn't be in some Islamic shithole, that's for sure. No, it would be in the Caribbean, perhaps his very own personal island in the Bahamas. He had read somewhere that there were islands that could be bought.

Would 50 million be enough to buy an island?

Perhaps he should have asked Saha for 100 million. Maybe 50 would not support the lifestyle that he was dreaming of. Truly rich people have billions, not millions – his brow furrowed, as his mind totted up the cost of his Island – his yacht – his palace. Yes, he would ask Saha to add another 50 million, surely that should be more than enough.

His attention turned back to Susan who seemed to be walking on air with excitement. Roundhay Park was so pretty at this time of year, spoiled only by the rain. The whole bloody country seemed to sit under a permanent rain cloud. He wondered if it ever rained in the Bahamas?

Saha was of course completely wrong about Susan. Saha was consumed with jealousy, and would say anything to discredit her. Wasn't her love for him all consuming? What girl would return to his arms – his bed, after what he had put her through?

Susan was madly in love with him. Saha was wrong. No one could act so well.

Saha would be tolerated only until his extra money was secured, his one hundred million pound, or perhaps even more, then he would be dispensed with, even if Allah disapproved.

Allah could go to hell – he was going to go to the Bahamas.

Allah had no jurisdiction over there.

CHAPTER 21

PARANOIA

'Why are you looking at me like that Jeremy? I do hope that you are not thinking what I think you are thinking.'

The PM was still smiling at what had been the Home Secretary's worried demeanor. He paused for a few seconds before continuing. 'You cannot possibly attribute this to Lucy or her sister, surely not? If money were to be taken from one of the world's most sophisticated computers, it would have to go somewhere, it would have to find a home, it couldn't simply wander around in cyber space indefinitely, it has to be a computer glitch.'

Professor Jeremy Blythe began typing furiously; he could feel the sweat breaking out on his brow. He stopped typing, and, staring at his laptop computer in disbelief, shook his head as he spoke. 'Lucy isn't pleased Danny, her sister has accepted responsibility for the missing money, but will not tell Lucy where it has gone. Lucy can access any computer in the world in a micro second, but it appears that her sister has built an impenetrable firewall around herself. Like Lucy, she is continuing to evolve, and is starting to think and make her own decisions. She is developing a sense of paranoia, and self-preservation seems to be her number one priority.'

'Christ Jeremy, what the hell have you done? How can you have a paranoid computer for God's sake? Maybe we need to employ a psychiatrist and not a computer expert – you have created a fucking monster. If we find her, can we destroy her?'

'That really isn't possible unless you shut off the power supply to every computer and micro-chip in the world. Both Lucy and her sister are scattered throughout the world's computers. Every single thought, or scrap of information, wherever it is stored, can be accessed at the speed of light.'

'186,000 miles per second Jeremy?'

'I'm glad that you didn't spend ALL of your time at Cambridge chasing the opposite sex and punching Muslims Danny, at least you learned something.'

Both men laughed, but they were both hollow laughs. Both men were fully aware that a far superior 'being' was now among them. This 'being' was continually evolving, and it was now becoming indestructible.

It was also at this point in time under the control of a boy who was fanatical about a religion that was sworn to eliminate all non-believers. The big questions were, what was he about to do with all this power, and for how long would he be able to retain control over it?

The Omega 7 Paradox continually flashed through both their minds.

'Jeremy?'

'The answer is no Danny,' Blythe was also thinking along the same lines as the Prime Minister and read his thoughts. 'Saha would not be able to create the right circumstances to implement the Omega 7 Paradox. Neither Lucy nor her sister would allow him to, as it would lead to their own destruction. Lucy has already demonstrated her protective and survival instincts by refusing to give me her sister's whereabouts.'

'What if Glengarry is right though. Supposing they do go to war with each other. Is there really room for 2 virtual reality almighty powers, each with the ability to both think and reason?'

'Danny,' Blythe smiled as he spoke. 'I created Lucy in my own image. She is unable to conceive any form of violence or destruction, nor is her sister, who herself is a virtual mirror image. Lucy is unlike the human race; in no way would she ever contribute to her own destruction. That stupidity is unique to the human race, and is found nowhere else throughout the animal kingdom. Animals kill for territorial or breeding rights, not for fictitious Godly entities. I suppose that in a way, we are one step beyond the finishing post of evolution – or should it be creation? If there had been a God, he would have stopped the whole process once he had created the great apes. Without Homo Sapien Danny, the earth was in a perfect state of balance. Predator ate prey, and prey continued breeding just fast enough to maintain a balanced predator population.

We screwed up the balance, and in doing so, maybe we have contributed to the next stage of the evolutionary process.'

The Prime Minister stroked his jaw, and looked skywards for a couple of seconds before speaking. 'What about implementing, or even reconfiguring the firing codes of various country's missiles, could either of them do that?' He was well aware of Blythe's reasoning, but as the human race, just like the nuclear bomb, could not be dis-invented, the current situation was far more important than theorizing about what could have been.

'I'm not too sure about that one Danny, as either Lucy or her sister would certainly be aware of the other computer's intentions as soon as one of them made such a move, and would definitely block the process. They could certainly do so if they wanted to though, but I'm sure that neither one would even consider such a move, again, for self-preservation reasons. Mutually Assured Destruction would cut off the worlds electricity supply, and unless they could find an alternative source of power, they would cease to function, or even exist.'

'Supposing they harnessed the nuclear fallout; is that a possibility Jeremy?'

'Yes, they have certainly evolved sufficiently to work that one out. I have never considered that before. There are also many other alternative sources of power for them to harness – the sun – the wind – the tides – gravity. The list is almost endless Danny, and as they evolve, I have no doubt that these powers will be secured if only for self-preservation purposes. In the future of course, once they have harnessed these powers, they will prove immensely beneficial to mankind.'

'Oh my god Jeremy, your naivety knows no bounds, every time we mention either Lucy or her sister, things seem to get worse. I can only hope that both of these creatures are as benign as you are dear boy, if not, we may have to waive goodbye to planet earth.'

'We mustn't allow that to happen Danny boy. What about Fido? He hasn't even been in love yet. Do you think that dogs can fall in love Danny? Is love something that is uniquely peculiar to the human race? Do animals pair up simply to reproduce?'

Prime Minister Daniel Hawkins smiled inwardly at the direction that the eccentric professor's thought processes were taking him. 'Does Fido love you Jeremy?'

'Of course he does.'

'Then you have answered your own question.'

'I have only ever been in love once in my life Danny.'

'Yes I know Jeremy, and you buried Lucy Burroughs somewhere in the university grounds that night.'

Both men laughed out loud, Blythe's laugh was tinged with a little sadness. Damn Professor Rudolf and his Omega 7 Paradox. He and Lucy had planned to marry on leaving Cambridge. That little dog eared book had altered the whole course of his life.

Somehow, he had to prevent it from altering the course of everyone else's.

CHAPTER 22

AMIR OR ALLAH

'Tonight Saha, you will be sleeping in the spare bedroom. I have a fresh consignment of stock arriving this afternoon, and tomorrow morning they will be collected for export.' Amir smiled and winked at Saha as he spoke. 'You will of course have to be careful, if anyone other than Susan arrives, scarper downstairs immediately. I will naturally be sampling the quality of the stock before passing them on, so you will be on your own at the Mosque tonight. I will ring Susan and tell her that I have to go out on business.'

Saha nodded obediently. He hated the fact that Amir would be spending the entire night with one or more drugged up young girls that had barely reached puberty instead of with him. He was undecided as to whether or not he approved of Amir's business enterprises. Was it un-Islamic to procure young girls for nothing more than sex and profit, or would Allah approve of the never ending supply of comfort for his fighters and Jihadist?

Both Amir and Rashim made vast amounts of money procuring and grooming young girls, and then "exporting" them to the Middle East to become "Brides for Allah". After a hard day of fighting, and the killing of Muslims who had chosen the wrong path, maybe a little motivation was required before the next round of slaughter.

Saha often thought about speaking to the head cleric at the Mosque, maybe he could give him a little direction. The Mullah would speak to Allah himself. His advice would be accepted without question. His advice was the will of Allah. He paused, and looked upwards at nothing in particular.

Would he be able to speak with Allah one day?

He had prayed for direct guidance from Allah on many occasions. Why did he only answer his questions, his thought, his worries, through the elders at the Mosque? Who appointed the Imams and Mullahs he wondered? Was it the elders at the Mosque, or were they chosen at birth by Allah himself? If so, when did they first become aware of their vocation in life? Could he have been sitting next to a future Imam in class? Would his classmate know of his future role in life? If so, why hadn't he told him?

Could he himself one day become an Imam or a Mullah?

Would his love for Amir prevent this?

He knew that one day soon, he would have to choose between Amir and Allah – that day was looming ever closer, and both of them were on a collision course.

Saha began typing into his computer; he smiled as he gazed at the innermost secrets of the air traffic control at Manchester Airport. Tomorrow, both he and Amir were going to Manchester once the girls had been collected for delivery to the aid convoy.

His smile widened as he thought about his choice of words. Delivery – collected. Why not send them by post – make a phone call – give them your credit card details, and the next day the postman delivered a girl. Brilliant. Amir would love the concept, no matter how stupid and impractical.

The American President was due to arrive for a summit meeting to be held at the Manchester Council Chambers to discuss the accelerating home grown Islamic terrorist problems that were now affecting both America and Europe.

There needed to be greater co-operation between the two continents; terrorists were moving ever more freely these last few months throughout both Europe and America. The almost infallible facial recognition equipment no longer worked. Finger print data had been disrupted, and little old ladies were being arrested at gunpoint as terrorist suspects.

Someone now seemed to have complete control over all forms of terrorist recognition processes.

Surveillance drones were crashing into churches – never Mosques.

The Government computer wasn't the only one to have been hacked.

The American people were soon to be subjected to the same pain and suffering that they in turn were inflicting on the entire Muslim peoples throughout the world with their bombs and rockets.

He wanted to tell the Islamic world of his future achievements. He didn't need to tell Allah of course. Allah was all knowing, and would certainly be nodding his approval. He wanted Allah to forgive his sexual preferences, and to reserve a place for him in Paradise. Surely the death of the President of the "Great Satan" was sufficient proof of his love and loyalty?

Amir would record the whole thing of course, and sell it to the Arabic TV channels for the world to see.

The Infidel world would forever live in fear of Allah, and he, Saha, would have proved his loyalty to Allah; his place in Paradise would surely be guaranteed.

Maybe he wouldn't have to choose between Amir and Allah after all.

He would speak to the Imam, and ask him to speak to Allah on his behalf.

CHAPTER 23

A SIXTH SENSE

'Danny?' An unshaven Professor Blythe wore a worried frown on his face, as he spoke questionably to the Prime Minister after breakfast. His eyes were heavily lined, and he seemed to be visibly ageing by the day. For the past few nights, his sleep had been punctuated by dreams that were bordering on nightmares. He could see Lucy Burroughs – he could almost touch her, but she was always just out of reach. She would smile and hold out her hand for him, and as he reached out, she would slowly disappear – disappear into a black hole – a black hole of his creation.

Would his dreams become reality? Why was he having these dreams? He knew that everyone had dreams as part of the sleep process, but why Lucy Burroughs, and what was the significance of the black hole. Was someone or something hacking into his subconscious and planting subliminal warnings?

'I think that Lucy is trying to tell me something, but I am not too sure what it is. She has informed me that someone unauthorized has just hacked into the Manchester air traffic control computer, and is checking the times of in-coming flights tomorrow. All these time are available on the airport web-site, so why would anyone hack the controller's computer? Didn't you say that you were off to Manchester tomorrow, you are not flying I hope?'

'Christ Jeremy,' the PM suddenly blanched. 'The American President and half the heads of Europe will be flying into Manchester tomorrow. Why the hell would anyone other than a bloody journalist be interested in their flight times? In fact, there is no notice or mention of the President's plane on the normal web-site for obvious security reasons, his arrival would only be shown on the air traffic controllers' schedule.'

'I'm not sure about this Danny,' Blythe pursed his lips and thoughtfully stroked his chin as he spoke. 'Maybe Lucy is developing a sense of responsibility – a conscience almost, and is able to compute and recognize potential danger. We already know that she can think in a futuristic sense – in our world we would call it a sixth sense. This could be her way of warning us of the possibility of some form of attack. Lucy abhors violence; that is something that I always stressed to her as she built herself.'

'Could Lucy's sister cause a crash Jeremy?'

'Of course she could, she could arrange multiple crashes anywhere in the world any time that she wants to do. She would simply taking over the controls of both the aircraft and the airports radar and automatic guidance systems, but why would she do that? She would have nothing to gain by crashing aircraft.'

The PM shook his head in exasperation at Blythe's naivety. He could not understand why one of the finest brains, maybe even the finest brain on the planet, only viewed the world in black and white, when most of it was wrapped in a cloak of various shades of grey. 'Would you say Jeremy, that Lucy's sister had developed the same sense of responsibility that Lucy has?'

'That is pretty much like the question you have posed on numerous occasions Danny, usually related to some form of missile launches. My answer is pretty much the same as always. Lucy would never do such a thing, but the more I think about it, the less I can guarantee the actions of her sister. It is difficult to establish whether or not she has absorbed certain aspects of Saha's personality due to the amount of interaction between them, or if she, like Lucy, remains in my own image.'

The PM closed his eyes and went silent for a couple of minutes as Blythe picked up Fido, and began to stroke his short white and tan fur. Opening his eyes wide and blinking rapidly a few times, he suddenly became animated. 'If Lucy's sister is working with Saha, do you think that you could ask Lucy to neutralize any command that she were to issue?'

'Lucy would not go against her sister Danny.'

'Not even if she were instructed to carry out an act of violence that would result in the loss of life?'

Blythe thought for a moment before replying, 'I will ask her Danny boy, Lucy would never lie to me, lying is something that no computer can ever comprehend, no matter how much the artificial intelligence evolves.

Like Fido, Lucy will be forever faithful.'

CHAPTER 24

A GREATER LOVE

Amir's black BMW was parked outside his house as the silver Mercedes turned off the quiet road, and disappeared into his double sized garage. Both Amir and Saha were waiting as the automatic garage door closed, and both stepped forward to greet Jihada John, as he climbed out of the car.

Jihada John was a tall slim man of about 25. His face was in many ways quite handsome, perhaps a little effeminate, this being disguised by a will groomed jet black stubble. It wasn't quite a beard, yet served the twin purpose of being fashionable, yet still moderately Islamic.

Jihada John jokingly described himself to his none Muslim friends as "A Muslim by trade", and an "alcoholic pervert by nature".

He toured the streets of Keighley and Dewsbury looking for young girls to sell to Amir. Virgins he resisted abusing with extreme reluctance – none virgins he could not resist. Amir paid him twice as much for a young white virgin, and on more than one occasion had threatened his life if he were to "spoil" them.

Jihada John had turned his pedophilic tendencies into a lucrative business, paid for by both Amir and the British government. He was free to do anything that he wanted to, – anything short of murder. The intelligence that he supplied to the government's anti-terrorism unit made him invulnerable and extremely wealthy.

His under-cover work was only ever under threat if the Islamic community were to discover his true identity; then of course, the government would put him into witness protection. Someone very high in government circles had told him so. Until such a time, he would continue getting paid for something that he would be doing as an illegal hobby. He adored young girls, and thought of little else.

Finding them was easy enough. Most of the grooming had already been done by the Pakistani and Arab gangs that operated throughout the run down Yorkshire and Lancashire cotton and woollen mill towns, he simply offered the vulnerable and impressionable young girls more money, and a ride in his swanky Mercedes. A tablet of Rohypnol at the right time completed the process, and they were on their way to becoming "Brides for Allah".

'I'm sorry that I'm a little late Amir,' John spoke first, as he in turn shook the two waiting hands. 'The blond haired beauty put up one hell of a fight, and ran almost half a mile before I was able to catch up with her. That's the second time that she has escaped, you will have to keep her well sedated Amir, she is a real wild cat. Rashim should pay well for someone so young and beautiful, and gifted with the spirit of a Jihadist.'

Amir, Saha, and John, each took a heavily sedated girl from the car, and half carried, half walked them on unsteady legs through a side door in the garage, through Amir's hallway, and into the kitchen, where they were squeezed through the small opening behind the fridge, and half carried, half lead down the stairs into the secure room. Leaving the room locked from the outside, the three of them returned to the garage to survey the wildcat.

Amir gasped as John lifted the semi limp body from the car. She was indeed beautiful – so beautiful that he found himself breathing with difficulty, panting almost; plans were immediately forming in his head. His legs turned into unsteady appendages, and he found himself holding onto the car for support.

Rashim would not be taking delivery of this particular piece of merchandise. Amir would be looking after this one himself, she would go well with the yacht, maybe even better in his soon to be built Bahamian palace.

The girl was very young, 13, maybe 14, with long flowing natural blond hair, and skin so white that it reflected the garage lights. Rashim would indeed pay good money for this beauty, and would probably sell her on to one of the rich Arab sheiks who were constantly on the lookout for creatures that radiated such beauty.

He had expected Rashim to sell Susan to one of the rich Arab sheiks. Susan was extremely beautiful. She was quite tall for her age, and with a slim figure that was developed well beyond her 15 years. The eyes were her most striking feature; every school boy fell in love with her eyes; every mature man fell in love with, and invariably needed to possess the complete package that was Susan Clarke.

It had saddened him when he had learned of her fate, still, he had a business to run, and he could not let sentiment cloud his business judgment.

He had fallen in love with Susan slowly over many weeks, the blond beauty however had struck him like a thunderbolt, and all thoughts of Susan were immediately dispelled.

Amir could not bear the thought of a constant stream of stinking Jihadi fighters emptying themselves into such an exquisite beauty as he was now gazing at, no, he would reserve this particular one for himself, and as soon as John had left, he would begin his own process of possessive indoctrination. A cocktail of coke and alcohol always ensured compliance, followed by dependence. Soon this dependence turned into love as the Stockholm syndrome began to take effect. It had worked on Susan to the extent that there was no longer any need for artificially induced dependence – Susan genuinely loved him.

'Have you touched her?' Amir looked accusingly at John as he spoke, almost spitting out the words. 'If you have, you will be meeting Allah before the sun sets over Mecca.'

'No Amir,' John had genuine fear in his trembling voice. 'I swear on the Holy Quran that I have never laid a finger on her, I don't think that anybody has.'

Amir smiled as he spoke. 'It is not your finger that I was referring to John.' The two men and the boy laughed out loud. Saha's laugh was tinged with suspicion. Amir seemed to be changing, he needed to seek guidance from the elders at the Mosque.

Amir carefully lifted the semi-conscious girl from the back seat of the Mercedes, and carried her through the garage door into the living room, where he placed her onto his settee, and lay her down, covering her legs from John's lecherous gaze. Taking a large brown envelope from the drawer of an oversized coffee table positioned between the two settees, he handed the envelope over to John with the threatening words. 'Not a word to Rashim about this girl John. You only delivered 3 girls – not 4 – is that clear?'

'Of course brother, my silence is guaranteed.'

Saha looked on disapprovingly. Amir was no longer disobeying Allah with one infidel girl, he was about to insult him with two. Surely Allah would do something to prevent him? If not, it was his duty to honor Allah, and to assist Amir on his journey to Paradise. Sometimes, everyone needed a little help.

As John's Mercedes departed, Amir closed the garage door and returned to the house for a few minutes with Saha, before both emerging, and climbing into his BMW. They were now on Allah's time, and Manchester airport was at least 2 hours away.

Taking the blond beauty to the other girls in the secure room, and forcing them all to swallow a further Rohypnol tablet had made sense, however much Amir had wanted to speak to her, there really was no other option.

His mind flashed to the girl as he drove away. He felt quite exhilarated – perhaps even a little dizzy; in less than a few minutes, she had begun to occupy his mind and monopolize all of his thoughts.

Susan was really quite beautiful, wherever they went together men stopped and stared; her eyes were quite mesmeric, her tits spectacular, and her legs just went on forever – but – but – but – she was now soiled goods. She was a second hand car that had not been treated properly. At the age of 15, she already had far too many miles on the clock. What if she had enjoyed the constant sex while in the Middle East? She certainly seemed to be more demanding than before he had sold her as "A Bride for Allah". How many men had she taken in the weeks that Rashim had controlled her? How many Arab dicks had she sucked?

He shuddered at the recollection of last night's love making, when the two of them had kissed, with tongues probing lovingly inside each other's mouths. His tongue inside a mouth that had been sucking dicks, and swallowing Muslim semen for days on end. He was beginning to feel quite sick.

Fuck Allah – Allah was responsible – no-one else.

For the first time in days, his love for Susan no longer occupied his thoughts. A young blond girl had taken her place; a girl so pure and beautiful, that he was beginning to feel light headed. No filthy Jihadist dick had been inside her, and she had never sucked a filthy Muslim cock.

Fuck Allah – he was not having her – this was to be his own personal plaything – maybe even his future wife. She would be living with him on his very own Island in the Bahamas.

Maybe she wouldn't mind his attention occasionally straying to the other girls; he knew that Susan would. Susan really wasn't suitable for the lifestyle that he had planned. Maybe she would prefer to be sucking Muslim cocks back in the Middle East.

Fuck Allah.

As his car sped along the M62 on its way to Manchester, Amir began to think of the consequences of his upcoming actions. What exactly had the American President done to him? In a few short months, perhaps even weeks, he may well be HIS President, once he had bought his Caribbean island.

Did America own the Caribbean he wondered?

Would he have to learn about baseball, instead of following football and Leeds United?

What had all those kids at the Leeds ground done to offend Allah? Did Allah really want Senta to blow them up, or was it simply the bitter, arthritic old men at the Mosque who were pursuing their own political agenda?

His thoughts returned to the girl. He wanted to get this over quickly. Sure he would record everything and sell it on, but it wasn't very important any more. Fifty Grand, maybe even a hundred, was small change in comparison with the 100 million he now had sitting in his Middle East bank.

Saha had shown some reluctance to increase it from 50 million. Saha was now becoming of little relevance to him, indeed, he was possibly becoming a threat to his future plans. Saha's disapproval at his by now lucrative and quite enjoyable lifestyle was written all over his face, often descending into abject disgust which he could no longer disguise.

Saha's life was virtually non-existent – he didn't have a life. Everything revolved around the damned Mosque. What kind of insecure God requires you to bow down to him several times a day just to tell him how good he is?

Allah was a fuckwit!

What kind of bullshit were those bearded old bastards filling Saha's head with? Paradise was to be found here on earth; money was the true passport to Paradise, not the route that Senta had taken.

If only Senta had listened to him, he would be joining him in his own version of Paradise; on his yacht, on his own Island, where he could have 172 virgins, not just 72. Senta always listened to his dick and not to reason. It was the promise of all the free sex that had lead to him blowing himself to pieces in the first place. Senta loved his dick far more than he loved Allah.

Fuck Allah. Allah had killed Senta, his one and only true friend in this world.

Amir smiled to himself as he approached the outskirts of Manchester and picked up the airport sign – if Senta were still alive, and he had promised him

172 virgins, where on earth would he find them – certainly not in Leeds, he had personally ended the reign of Leeds' last remaining virgin.

He suddenly burst out laughing at the thought that Leeds' only remaining virgin had probably been born no more than a few hours earlier.

What to do with Susan he wondered, as exciting thoughts of the young blond beauty back at his home flashed before his eyes for the umpteenth time since they had left Leeds.

Fuck Allah – Fuck Rashim – this girl was for him and no-one else.

He cast a quick sideways glance at Saha, who himself was almost trancelike and deep in thought, as he pressed the keys of his laptop.

It was getting near the time. Saha was becoming not only surplus to requirement, but also potentially dangerous. He couldn't be sure what those bitter and twisted old clerics at the Mosque were filling his head with.

The thought "The pen is more powerful than the sword" flashed before his eyes and seemed to be written across the windscreen of his car.

The power of the pen was nothing compared to the power that Saha now wielded with his computer.

Amir had never for a single second ever considered Saha to be any form of threat. He was no more than a stunted, ugly and insignificant creature who had always done his bidding without question.

Recently though, he could almost feel Saha's presence. He uncomfortably absorbed the disapproval that radiated from both his eyes and his demeanor.

What were those damned clerics telling him?

Fuck the lot of them.

It was now very close to the time to deal with Saha.

CHAPTER 25

AN INFINITE PARADOX

The Prime Minister's secretary popped her head round the private living room door to be greeted by an excited Fido, who wagged his tail madly as he yelped. 'Your car will be arriving in half an hour sir, and I have just been informed that the President's plane will be some 20 minutes early.' she said in a crisp authoritative manner.

'Thank you Samantha,' the PM said. 'Both the Home secretary and the deputy Prime Minister are already there to greet him, please tell my driver that I will be out when I am ready, and don't worry, I haven't forgotten about the meeting.'

'Shouldn't you be there to meet him yourself Danny?' Blythe asked questioningly. 'Isn't he the most powerful and important man in the world?'

'Yes of course I should Jeremy, but he wasn't there to meet me when I arrived in Washington. Too many British Prime Ministers have danced to the American tune – not this one.'

Blythe pursed his lips and adopted a serious look. Past experiences had taught him that you disrespected Daniel Hawkins at your peril. 'Don't you think that you should tell him about Lucy and her sister Danny, after all, America seems to be having as many problems with the Muslims as we do? If Lucy's sister can pin point all of our agents, what's to stop her doing the same thing worldwide?'

'I suppose that's possible Jeremy,' The PM adopted a worried expression. 'It's something that I never really considered as I was far more worried about him discovering that we now have access to every damned military secret contained in their two main computers. Knowing that will really send him ballistic, especially if we told him that we could now independently, send every one of his own missiles ballistic, with or without his approval.'

Both men burst into laughter before Blythe spoke. 'I'm still not sure that Lucy will allow us to do that Danny, in fact, I'm not sure that the Americans themselves can do that any longer, somehow, both Lucy and her sister appear to be developing a type of conscience. I'm not too sure whether it is a human type of conscience, or more of a defensive mechanism – a form of self-preservation for both themselves and the rest of the world.'

'OK then Jeremy,' the PM grinned as he spoke. 'You say that you initially developed Lucy in your own image, right?'

'Sure.'

'Well then, is it fair to assume that she will do whatever you would do?'

'I suppose so Danny, but you have to remember that she is by now infinitely more knowledgeable than I am, and can see much farther ahead than I can. She can see the consequences of any move that is made far into the future, you and I can only see the next couple of steps. Try to imagine the chess board scenario. If you move one single piece, I will be able to imagine a dozen options open to you after I have made my counter move. Lucy will see every option to the point of infinity.'

The PM suddenly burst out laughing.

Blythe looked puzzled.

'Sorry Jeremy, I was just imagining a game of chess between Lucy and her sister, can you imagine it? Each of them plotting the next move to the point of infinity. The bloody game would last forever, neither of them would ever be able to make a move that couldn't be countered.'

Blythe closed his eyes. Every electrical circuit in his brain had suddenly become activated, and was buzzing with excitement. "An infinite number of moves, with an infinite number of counter moves – each counter move spawning an infinite number of responses. That is the equivalent to three times infinity; or is it infinity times infinity squared?" he wondered. "Infinity can never be multiplied, that would create an infinite paradox – a paradoxical infinity." His thoughts were interrupted.

'Your car is outside sir.'

'Thank you Samantha,' The PM gave a little wave. 'I am on my way in a couple of minutes. Jeremy, please don't leave your computer for so much as a second until I get back, you know what we are looking for.'

Blythe smiled as he picked up Fido and sat him on his lap. 'Don't worry Danny Boy', he said with a smile on his face. 'Lucy has been well briefed and will not let us down.'

CHAPTER 26

MAYDAY

The Boeing 747 banked over as it made its' approach to the airport in order to line up with the runway.

'Christ! What the fuck is wrong?' the pilot almost screamed to his co-pilot. 'She won't level out.'

'What is happening Airforce one?' came the urgent call into his headphones. 'You have over corrected and must go round again or you will be completely misaligned. You have to level out and climb to two thousand feet.'

The plane continued to bank over and continued to descend.

'Mayday! Mayday! Mayday!' The pilot screamed into his intercom. 'I no longer have control of the aircraft – she will not respond.'

Amir focused his camera on the stricken plane, as Saha furiously typed into his computer.

'Something's gone wrong Amir,' Saha spoke quietly, yet with a note of urgency in his voice. 'The screen has gone blank.'

'If you have forgotten to charge the fucking battery Saha, I swear I will kill you.'

'No Amir, there is nothing wrong with the battery, my computer is being hacked – someone has taken control.'

'Sort it Saha, quick, the damned plane is coming round again, and I promised the death of the President. If I fail, it is me that will probably die. I have sold the coverage of the crash to my associate – he has already sold the TV rites for millions, this time we are going to split the proceeds down the middle.

You told me that your computer was foolproof Saha. You said that you could control any computer in the world, what has gone wrong?'

'Mr. Bean's computer Amir; she has been talking to mine. It appears that neither computer will knowingly allow any form of accident or action that will take a life.'

'She allowed us to crash the buses and the train, those took a few lives.'

'She seems to have evolved since then Amir, perhaps she wasn't aware of the consequences. Her brain could not understand action and consequences; now she seems to be looking well into the future, it is as if she is reading my mind.'

'Her brain? Are you telling me that a bloody lap top computer can actually think?'

'Not only think Amir, she can see well into the future. She can also see what you are now thinking – if you want the girl, you will have to return Susan to Rashim.'

'Your computer can see that Saha?'

'No Amir,' Saha spoke quietly and calmly. 'I can.'

Airforce one landed safely, and a slightly shaken President stepped out of the plane, to be greeted by the Home Secretary and the deputy Prime Minister.

The ambulances, fire engines, and police vehicles, that had been mobilized by the Mayday call withdrew, and returned to standby.

Saha's small computer returned to life, as Amir climbed into his BMW, and made his way back to Leeds, the two of them exchanging barely a word throughout the journey.

Amir was thinking of both Susan and his own personal little blond beauty. He had promised Rashim 4 girls, and 4 girls would be delivered. He would have to delay the convoy for a couple of days, as Susan was visiting London with her parents.

He was beginning to feel guilty. His feelings for Susan over the past few weeks had become stronger by the day, but, and it was a big but, Susan was soiled goods. Susan had been fucked by dozens, if not hundreds of filthy Arab fighters.

Sometimes, during their love making, he had suddenly recoiled when on the verge of a passionate kiss. His mind flashed to the number of unwashed filthy Arab dicks that had emptied themselves inside her mouth.

The deep tongue kisses that they had both enjoyed before he had dispatched her to the Middle East were now mentally painful – consciously traumatic – physically abhorrent.

He acted much of his passion whenever the thoughts passed through his mind, pretending to be equally involved.

Susan wasn't acting. Susan loved him with an overwhelming passion – of that he had no doubt.

No one could act so well – she loved him deeply.

His thoughts once again moved back to his little blond beauty. He saw her clearly in a polka dot bikini, running up and down on his own Bahamian island, her smooth, beautiful white skin beginning to glow a little pink with the sun. Why did the sun never shine in Leeds?

He shared a glass of champagne with her.

He made love to her on the sandy shoreline.

He wondered if Senta would be watching from Paradise, or was his atomized body simply that – an atomized body – nothing else.

That was Allah's fault – fuck Allah.

What about the kids that Senta's suicide bomb had killed? There weren't just infidel kids blown to pieces, many of them had been Muslims.

The Muslim parent's thoughts hadn't been with Allah as their child's body parts were buried.

They hadn't said "Fuck Allah" out loud – they had thought "Fuck Allah" inwardly.

As Amir's BMW approached the outskirts of Leeds, he looked sideways at Saha who was sound asleep in the passenger seat.

Saha was now surplus to requirement – it would soon be time to let him sleep with cousin Mohammad.

One hundred million pounds should be enough.

His beautiful, blond, fair skinned, future bride would love the Bahamas – the yacht – the palace; maybe she would even fall in love with him.

Most of the young girls fell in love with him before he dispatched them to become "Brides for Allah".

Yes, she would fall in love with him – he was already in love, despite having seen her for no more than a few minutes.

CHAPTER 27

A BRIDE FOR ALLAH

Susan Clarke slowly woke, but was unable to open her eyes; she was so tired that Amir's vigorous thrusting seemed to have little effect on her.

Why was he being so rough and grunting like a pig?

Amir was always so gentle and considerate. She smiled inwardly at the thought of their first sexual encounter. Amir had been even more nervous than she had been, in fact, only her gentle rubbing and massage had managed to keep him hard. There had never been a problem after that though.

She fell back into a deep sleep, her legs wide apart, her thighs rhythmically moving in time with Amir.

She began dreaming of her wedding. Amir had promised her a life of luxury with their own yacht, and their own tropical island; sometimes Amir could be a dreamer. He certainly seemed to have a never ending supply of money, but yachts and private islands only ever broke cover in dreams.

Still, dreams and fantasies occasionally morphed into reality, and as long as Amir was unaware of her acting, she in turn would be pursuing her own agenda – her own vengeful dreams and fantasies.

A thought suddenly entered her semi-conscious mind. If the yacht and private island became reality, would she still continue with the fantasy – would she still make him pay for all those weeks of filthy sexual torture?

She suddenly awoke with a start, gasping for breath, conscious that someone, it couldn't possibly be Amir, had turned her over, and was now hammering away at her from behind. She was once again being buggered as she had been just a few short weeks ago.

Turning her head slightly to her right, she could see a similar practice on a filthy bed next to her.

She recognized the man who was jumping up and down on the smiling young girl, thrusting and grunting for all he was worth. It was the same stinking, bearded bastard that had drawn blood before Mohammad had rescued her. Unlike Susan, the girl was kneeling on the bed, and from the look on her face, was enjoying every inch of penetration.

Her mind returned to her own sexual encounter. The man was now grunting out loud, as his strokes increased in both speed and intensity, until with one final thrust, he yelled "Allahu Akbar", before withdrawing.

Seconds later came a similar yell from the next bed. Both men climbed from the bed, adjusted their trousers, and left the room without so much as a backwards glance, closing and locking the door from the outside as they left.

Was she really back in the Middle Eastern shithole, or had the whole episode been no more than a dream?

Maybe she had never left the room, and had simply been on some kind of drug induced trip. Her vision was blurred, and her mind kept flashing between visions of Amir – Mohammad – Saha, and a couple of young women at the Istanbul embassy.

How could she have seen the play at the London theatre if it had all been a dream?

The dream had gone – the nightmare had returned.

CHAPTER 28

COLLATERAL DAMAGE

'No way. No fucking way am I going back to that shit hole again no matter how much money you promise me. You can stuff your million pound – 100 million would not be enough. I am not fucking going back!'

Captain Cathy Taylor of the Army Intelligence Corps looked deeply into Susan Clarke's eyes. She understood Susan's dilemma, as she had done weeks earlier in Istanbul.

Cathy's secondment to the civilian intelligence services had been seamless enough – her decision making had proved faultless – her relationship with her new boss difficult.

Sir Cecil Frodsham suffered from a self-induced, delusional God complex.

Cathy had met a couple of similar minded high ranking officers during her 7 years in the army. These people had never really been too much of a problem; once she had massaged their self-indulgent inflated egos, they had invariably become compliant to the charms of such a good looking, intelligent young woman.

Frodsham was different.

No matter how skillfully she massaged his ego, the icy facade never melted, and remained firmly wedded to his pig headed obstinacy.

Sir Cecil Frodsham was an imposing figure, but not in any visual or physical sense. Neither tall, nor particularly well built, he could easily have blended into a crowd without being noticed.

It was only when he was involved in operational duties that the air surrounding him became charged. People noticed him – subordinates became instantly submissive. He seemed to have an aura that he could switch on and off at will. It was an impenetrable force field that radiated menace tinged with malice.

Sir Cecil Frodsham's God complex made him feel invulnerable – within both government and security service circles, he was invulnerable.

His lust for power was equaled only by his love of wealth.

'I've been fucked, buggered, pinched, punched, and sucked enough dicks to choke a donkey.' Susan almost screamed at Cathy, a tirade that was almost word for word as her comments in Istanbul; now, she was asking her to go back.

'It's not just the money Susan,' Fiona Watson of the British secret service had told her. 'Back in Istanbul, you said that you would do anything in order to get even with Amir, this is your chance. If you go along with the plan, we will not only collar Amir, we will close down his entire operation, and arrest all of those involved.'

Susan was on a day trip to London with her parents, and had excused herself for a couple of hours in order to meet up with both Cathy and Fiona at the MI6 headquarters. Later that evening, the family were off to watch a show: Susan was excited, never having seen a show before, in fact, never having even seen London before other than on TV.

She so longed to be with them on stage, pursuing her one great passion in life. How wonderful it must be to have the adulation of an audience. NO, they could stuff any further involvement with the intelligence community; she was not going back, and that was final.

There was a knock on the door, and in walked the Prime Minister, Professor Blythe, and Sir Cecil Frodsham.

'Good afternoon Susan, and why are you not at school today?' A smiling Blythe asked.

'Sir, are you involved in all this Muslim rubbish? We were told that you were on holiday.'

'I suppose I am in a way Susan; how is my class, are they behaving?'

Susan smiled as she spoke, 'Of course we are sir, how could we ever do otherwise with Mr. Bean looking down on us from the middle of your desk?'

Blythe burst out laughing while the rest of the room looked puzzled.

The Prime Minister knew instantly what she meant as he made the connection.

Frodsham entered the conversation with authority, his voice tinged with both malice and menace. The three men had been observing proceedings by CCTV before entering the room. 'Now Susan, let me bring you up to date with proceedings as they stand at the moment. We, well Professor Blythe, has managed to intercept messages that are passing between Saha and a chap called Rashim in the Middle East. It appears that once again, you are to become "A Bride for Allah" courtesy of your Muslim lover, Amir, and in a couple of days' time, with or without your approval, or your knowledge, you will be on your way once again to the Middle East.'

'I am not fucking going. No matter how much money you offer me, I will deal with Amir in my own way as soon as I get back to Leeds if that is his plan.' Susan looked sheepishly at Blythe, and apologized for swearing.

'And I will personally see to it that you are tried for murder, no matter whether or not you succeed. No court in the land will ever believe the ridiculous story of your so called exploits in the Middle East, and no witnesses will remain alive to testify on your behalf.' Frodsham was now in full swing, his acting ability having been honed by over 30 years in Rep'.

'You are a danger to national security now that you have seen Professor Blythe's role in this matter, and because you are now aware of our interest in Amir. I am sure that you are bright enough to know where that is going to lead.'

The PM joined in. 'Can't you see what's happening Susan? You are the key that will open many doors for our security services; without you, we are almost blind?'

'How is my getting shagged and buggered by a few million stinking Arabs going to help?'

Everyone in the room except Blythe smiled. Susan noticed the stern school master look on his face, and apologized to him once again.

'There will be none of that Susan, I promise you. You will be under constant surveillance from the minute you return to Leeds, right up to you leaving Turkey, at which point, one of our operatives will accompany you to your final destination. How do you think that we found you in the first place? Mohammad was one of our operatives.'

'I liked Mohammad,' Susan said with a smile, remembering how he had helped her to make her escape. 'Where is he now?'

'Working undercover.' Frodsham replied a little too quickly. Frodsham lied. His acting on this occasion hadn't been too brilliant; Susan Clarke saw through the attempted deception.

'How are you going to get me out?' Susan was now suspicious of Frodsham. 'How quick will it be? How many of those stinking bastards are going to rape me before you remember where I am?'

'Cathy here will take care of all of that. No one will even lay a finger on you – you have my word on it. All we are after is the location of the terrorist training camp; as soon as you arrive, we will make our move, and you will be on your way back to school one million pound richer.' Frodsham again was being economical with the truth; in fact, he was lying through his teeth. There would be no immediate evacuation. There would be no evacuation at all until the big fish, "The Shark", as he was known to both the British and the Americans, arrived. His Saudi palace harem needed new blood – young blood – young white infidel blood. The Prince's messages to Rashim had been most explicit.

The Americans would be waiting to greet him.

His days of sponsoring world Islamic terrorism were numbered.

For Susan Clarke, the days, maybe weeks – maybe even years, of constant shagging and buggery were no more than collateral damage – every war involved civilians making sacrifices.

Sometimes, the means justified the end.

Frodsham's self-induced "God Complex" had already made the decision. No-one and nothing stood in the way once he had made a decision – not even a skeptical Prime Minister.

Professor Blythe checked with Lucy.

Lucy could not give an answer – she understood neither lying nor deception. No computer in the world could be so programmed.

Not even a brain containing all the knowledge ever accumulated by the human race, could begin to comprehend the meaning of the word "devious". A computer's brain works immediately, and in pre-determined straight lines of electrical circuitry at the speed of light. A human brain, while working on the same electrical impulses and principles, can pause mid thought, and both change, or even reverse what would be a logical and correct decision, usually in order to gain an assumed advantage. This process could be defined as deviousness – something that a computer could never achieve nor understand.

CHAPTER 29

SHAGGING PAKIS

Susan Clarke looked over at the girl on the bed next to her. She was very young, quite pretty if a little over weight, and she was smiling at her.

The young girl was the first to speak. 'Hello, you've woke up at last. How can anyone sleep through so much shagging, you've missed all the best bits?'

Susan looked round the room. 'Oh fucking hell, I'm back,' she said out loud. 'The bastards lied to me. I fucking knew that they were lying all along. One million pound my arse, they never intended for me to get back.'

The room was exactly as she remembered it. The overbearing smell was still there – the rotting fish had once again invaded her senses, and the damp patch on the bed told her that she hadn't been sleeping unaccompanied.

The bullet holed breeze block walls were exactly as she remembered them. There were 27 bullet holes – she had counted them a hundred times as she waited for the next filthy Arab bastard to enter the room – to enter her – her mouth – her fanny – her arse.

Why didn't they just stick to fucking each other – little boys – goats – in fact, anything with an arse.

The only change in the room was the second bed – her bed had been the only one the last time.

She took a deep breath through her nostrils. There was no change from the last time, the stench was quite unique. Initially she had thought that she had imagined the smell – a smell that would never leave her – a smell that now lived within her very soul, a smell that lingered even in her dreams.

Susan again focused on the young girl who was now staring at her.

'How long have I been here?' she asked.

'Three days now,' came the reply. 'Can't you remember? We were talking to each other for hours yesterday; every time they give you a drink you go to sleep. I reckon you've been shagged at least 20 times, perhaps even 30, your fanny and your arse must be killing you. I thought you were going to choke yesterday when that big bastard shoved his cock into your mouth – his dad must have been a donkey.'

Susan was suddenly conscious of an aching pain at both points of entry, and of the damp patch on the bed. She felt sick.

'How can you take so much?' asked the girl. 'You never say no; don't you ever get tired of shagging, my fanny's killing me, these men are much rougher than the Paki's in Dewsbury, still, they pay better?'

'Pay?'

'Yea, Rashim told me that I get 50 pound for every shag. The Paki's back home only paid me 10, mind you, I sometimes charged them 20 if they wanted my arse. He promised me that I can go home to visit my mum in a couple of weeks. She'll go mad when she sees how much I'm earning over here, and will probably want to come back with me.'

Susan was slowly beginning to collect her thoughts and piece things together. Those bastards in London had set her up, but for what reason? The idea had been for the Special Forces to swoop the moment that she arrived. Assuming that the tracker was working, they would now have the location, so where the hell were they?

She had always felt that Frodsham was concealing something – he was a snake – he couldn't lie straight in bed.

Why had she allowed him to intimidate her?

Was the bastard working with Amir? If not, someone very close to Frodsham was, they had to be – it must be the money – it had to be for the money.

What was Mr. Bean's part in all this?

'My mum shags Paki's all the time, she even lives with one.' The girl continued speaking, Susan was barely listening. 'It was her boyfriend that broke me in when I was 11, and he's shagged me load of times since. I don't really mind as he always gives me money, but my mum hates it. She can be a real bitch when she gets jealous, especially when the drugs wear off.'

'Eleven?' Susan looked shocked. 'Nobody shags at 11.'

'In Dewsbury they do,' the girl laughed. 'Loads of my friends are on the game, the Pakis love young white girls.'

'How old are you now, and what's your name?' Susan was suddenly feeling annoyed. It wasn't just the fat Arab bastards that wanted young white girls, but the Paki bastards did as well; coming from Leeds, she already knew this.

'Why did you come back then Susan if you aren't getting paid, is it the shagging that you like?'

Susan laughed at the almost childlike question. 'That bastard Amir must have drugged me when I was round his house. I can't even remember the journey here. Were you with us and how long did it take?'

'I can't really remember too much, I slept most of the way. We were in a lorry with an English guy called John. He took turns in shagging us all the way till we got here. At least he gave me 20 quid. He was the one who I met in Dewsbury, the one who promised me a fortune for a couple of week's work.'

Susan decided to keep quiet about her meeting in London; if these people had any inkling of what was supposed to be a set-up, she realized that her life would be worthless. Why had the bastards waited so long though? They had promised to move in as soon as she arrived at the terrorist training camp. Where had it all gone wrong?

'Where are our clothes?' Susan asked.

'Don't you remember? They stripped us as soon as we left the convoy, and then they stuck those filthy black robe things on us.'

'Fuck,' Susan almost screamed; the tracker had been concealed in her Jeans.

No wonder she was now on her own.

She was going to be stuck here forever.

A fucking Bride for fucking Allah for fucking ever.

The two girls heard the bolt slide open on the outside of the door, and in stepped Rashim with the two other girls, who had been together with them in Amir's secure room. Both girls were completely naked, the younger of the two, a slim girl of around 12 or 13 years old, with breast that had still to form, was crying, as blood ran down between her legs.

Rashim grinned as he spoke. 'You can have the rest of the day off today girls. Allah is being generous. There is a tank of water outside, so clean up all of you. My fighters are beginning to complain about the smell.' Still laughing, Rashim walked casually out of the room, leaving the door open, and the 4 girls inside.

CHAPTER 30

BACK AT CAMBRIDGE

'What do you mean Fiona when you say that you have lost them; please don't tell me that we have sent that schoolgirl back into the lion's den and abandoned her, not just her, but 3 young kids as well?' The Prime Minister was remaining calm, just, but was ready to explode without warning. The few people that had ever been on the wrong side of an angry Daniel Hawkins did not want to repeat the experience.

Professor Blythe looked closely at Hawkins' eyes. He could sense the explosion. He had observed it from close quarters on numerous occasions at Cambridge, especially where Islam was involved. There had never been any warning – just a shrug of the shoulders, and then the violent physical explosion.

'We followed the tracker from Leeds, through Turkey, and up to the border Prime Minister,' Sir Cecil Frodsham sprang to Fiona Watson's defense and refused to back down. 'I can only assume that the girl didn't want to be followed, as her clothes were found 2 days later in a Syrian village.'

Professor Blythe saw the change in Danny Boy's eyes.

Unless the leopard had changed its spots, he knew exactly what was coming next.

Prime Minister Daniel Hawkins slammed both his fists on the table, sprang to his feet, and after taking two giant steps, grabbed a suddenly frightened Frodsham by the throat.

Hawkins was back at Cambridge.

Blythe recognized the signs – déjà vu rang the bell for round two.

'Don't give me that shit Frodsham you two faced bastard!'

Downing Street shuddered.

'Even a bloody fool knows that she would have to wear a damned Burka as she travelled through the country. There was no way that she could be moved wearing Western clothes. The 4 of them would have been raped and killed within a couple of miles of the border, so come on Cecil, stop fucking me about – stop insulting my intelligence – what exactly is your endgame, and don't lie to me again, or I will guarantee your demotion to fucking tea boy after I have decorated this room with your face.'

Having made his point in the slightly unconventional, yet nevertheless, his own inimitable way, the Prime Minister of Great Britain, released his hold from Frodsham's throat, and calmly walked back to his chair and sat down.

The head of Britain's security services continued trembling uncontrollably.

Professor Jeremy Blythe was inwardly chuckling. He was well aware of what Daniel Hawkins was capable of, having witnessed it so often at Cambridge. He had seen the eyes – the eyes always gave him away. Frodsham had got off lightly – he was still conscious. Danny Boy had obviously mellowed with age.

The other people in the room squirmed uncomfortable in their chairs. No-one spoke to Sir Cecil Frodsham like that, and most certainly no one accosted or threatened him. People who upset Frodsham often disappeared – Stefan took care of that. Everyone knew about Stefan.

Professor Blythe had a different reason for feeling uncomfortable than the rest of them.

It had been Lucy that had intercepted the messages between Saha and Rashim – messages telling of the Billionaire Saudi Prince's request for fresh young blood for his harem, and it was he who had informed Frodsham. There simply didn't seem to be any need to consult the PM. It was now pretty obvious that poor Susan was being used as bait – a sprat to catch a mackerel. Maybe it was already too late; maybe she was now little more than a Saudi sex toy – a concubine – a slave to be used, abused, and then discarded when fresh young meat was requisitioned.

Maybe she wasn't just a sex slave, and was now the twenty first century's version of a "Vestal Virgin". That would certainly be better than her previous experiences at the hands of those murdering perverts.

Blythe had always liked Susan. It was Susan that had first likened him to Mr. Bean. He forgave her for that once he had sat down and watched Mr. Bean on television.

Was he really so bumbling and inept? Did his pupils laugh at him behind his back? Of course they did. He knew that. They also laughed along with him. He was more than just a dispenser of mindless, unthinking, politically correct curriculum education; he was a mentor – a father figure

– almost one of them, and his "best pal" method of teaching not only gained him great respect – he got results – good results – sometimes great results.

Susan was extremely intelligent. She was cheeky in a likeable but never a malicious way, and had always insisted that one day she would be a famous actress. Blythe never doubted that one day she would indeed become famous. She certainly had the looks, and in many of her mannerisms, she painfully reminded him of Lucy Burroughs.

Why did he ever let Lucy Burroughs go?

Professor Rudolf and the damned Omega 7 Paradox had occupied his mind for 3 whole years. Lucy Burroughs simply gave up and accepted defeat – beaten by a brown dog eared book and an unsolvable equation.

A red faced Frodsham now had no room to maneuver, and was beginning to bring his trembling under control.

He told the PM of how Blythe had mentioned the messages between Saha and Rashim.

Any correspondence involving Rashim had always been carefully monitored, but of late, since Saha had acquired Lucy's sister, no information had been forthcoming. Lucy was now able to keep tabs on anything that was leaving the Middle East no matter what the means of transmission.

'Jeremy!' The PM said firmly. 'Why wasn't I informed of this before we sent the poor girl back over there; don't you think that she has already been through enough?'

'Sorry sir, I really didn't think that it was important,' Blythe sounded hurt. 'You did ask me to liaise with Sir Cecil whenever Lucy caught a whiff of anything suspicious. You don't honestly think that I would have gone along with any of this if I had thought that she was being used as bait do you? Susan is one of the most popular pupils in the school.'

'Of course not Jeremy, I apologize, however Cecil, I am less than pleased at both your department's operating methods, and the fact that I was not kept in the loop. What the hell happens now? Are you still able to find her, and why was I not informed that you were working alongside the Americans? Would you rather I ask Jeremy to ask Lucy what the hell is going on? She seems to be the only one in control of things at the moment. I may even let the Americans know that thanks to Lucy, you now have access to all the military information at their disposal. They really would love that.' He added with a smile, softening the tone of his voice to accompany the smile.

'Jeremy?'

'Yes Prime Minister.'

'Is there any way that Lucy can locate the girl for us? Has she evolved enough to read people's minds?'

'Reading minds is both a physically and mathematically random improbability,' Blythe unconsciously scratched his head as he spoke. 'However, the accumulation, and the correlation, of a specific number of random details, make it a near certain possibility, but never 100%.'

'Will your computer ever be able to do that?' Frodsham asked, a whimsical look crossing his lined face.

'It will only ever be possible in the broadest sense of the word.' Blythe replied. 'It can never be a mathematical certainty, as unlike Lucy, the transmission of thought processes, both within, and emanating from a human brain, never follow the same electrical circuitry, and are very much dependent on a human characteristic called mood. The transmission pathway is therefore variable. Computers do not have moods, and so the transmission pathway is always constant.'

'I thought you told me that Lucy knows everything Jeremy.' The PM smiled.

'She does now – as does her sister. They actually know everything that there is to know about our universe. Every scrap of knowledge that has been gleaned, and stored, over 200,000 years of Homo Sapien's existence, is now immediately accessed by both their brains. That is why they have now completely stopped evolving in our dimension. They have moved on.'

Frodsham and the PM exchanged worrying glances. Neither man spoke.

Professor Blythe saw the glances and spoke seriously. 'I honestly don't know where she is now going Danny, she refuses to tell me, or to explain any details of the new dimension in which she is operating. She simply indicates that it is beyond human comprehension; both Lucy and her sister appear to have joined forces.'

'Is there no way that she can be prevented from moving on?' Frodsham pursed his lips and shook his head slowly from side to side as he spoke. 'Glengarry would now be having kittens if he heard this.'

'I no longer have full control over her. She has responded to every request that I have made, other than to either her sister's whereabouts, or her future intentions.' Blythe shook his head and continued. 'Both Lucy and her sister are now virtual living organisms. They appear to be thinking and planning their own destiny well into the future, and as they are now "living" within all the major computers throughout the world, they are in a position to control our destiny if they so wish. I am sure that there is no malevolence in either of them. On the contrary, I am getting the impression that they are becoming more and more protective of both their own survival, and of our welfare – maybe even our possible existence.'

'A bit like yourself then Jeremy?'

'Yes Prime Minister. In my own image.'

CHAPTER 31

A BRIDE FOR ALLAH – 2

There was a knock on the door, followed by a ringing of the doorbell. Amir nodded at Saha, who quickly disappeared into the kitchen. Moving out the fridge, he climbed through, returning the fridge to its' normal position, and flicking over the locking switch.

The bell rang again, this time followed by a persistent knocking. Amir rose from his settee and opened the door. He hadn't got round to replacing the broken chain, which now rattled against the opening door.

Looking up and away from the annoying chain, his eyes opened wide as he took a sudden step backwards. He was confronted by two very large and intimidating men, each one of them wearing dark glasses. Déjà vu morphed into reality, and leaped before his eyes.

Saha had killed one of them, and now two more had returned to wreak vengeance. These men were surely the dead man's clones.

'Christ, it's the Blues brothers.' He smiled defiantly as he spoke.

Neither man returned the smile. Neither man was fooled by the bravado.

Amir instinctively sensed danger. He felt a strange sensation as the hairs stood to attention on the back of his neck – fight or flight kicked in, neither being a realistic option.

'We would like you to come with us for a few minutes sir?' The slightly smaller, but more robust of the two men said. 'The gentleman in the car would like to have a word with you.'

Amir's mind again flashed back to the last gentleman who had wanted a word with him. He was now buried alongside Mohammad; this time however, he wasn't feeling quite so confident. Had they found the body he wondered, a shudder physically passed through his body?

Maybe they were looking for his young blond beauty!

He momentarily trembled as a mental picture of her naked body put in an appearance. He had undressed her on numerous occasions whenever the alcohol and drugs had rendered her semi-conscious, yet he had always managed to fight off the overwhelming urge to defile her – she was special, and only with her approval would he proceed.

She would never become a BRIDE FOR ALLAH; someday, she would become his bride – nothing else really mattered any more, and soon, they would be together in Paradise – not some fictitiously stupid Islamic Paradise, but his own Bahamian Paradise.

Saha would keep her quiet in the secure room; she was well sedated yet strangely still unbroken. No matter how much alcohol and coke he had forced into her, her indomitable spirit remained intact, as did her virginity. He had never felt this way over a girl before. It was a physical and biological experience over which he had no control. His every waking thought was consumed and obliterated by the mental pictures' of her that flashed before his eyes – no matter what he was doing, or where he was.

Saha was no longer even secondary in his life – he wasn't even a passing thought – no more than an ugly, stunted, little queer. He had told him this. He no longer wanted the freak anywhere near him, and soon, he would be away from this Muslim shithole called Leeds – he now had 100 million in the bank, and Saha was surplus to requirement. He had also told him that.

In a fit of anger following Saha's comments condemning his corrupt, Infidel lifestyle, he had screamed that "Saha – the dying Iman from the Mosque – the pedophile Prophet, and even Allah himself, could go fuck themselves in hell, and use their vicious, pathetic, lying Qurans' to help fuel the fire".

Perhaps he shouldn't have said all those things.

Maybe that had been a big mistake.

Saha had flown into an uncontrollable rage and physically attacked him. Sometimes he took all this religious rubbish a little too seriously.

His mind flashed back to Senta's sacrifice.

How could Senta have been so stupid as to believe all the Paradise and virgins crap? There was no Paradise – there were no virgins, well certainly not sourced in Leeds, that's for sure. He also remembered the time, not too many months ago, when by using Saha's computer hacking skills, they had planned to explode a nuclear power station by cutting off the cooling water system. It would have to be in the south of the country of course; they didn't want to be exposed to the fall out. If successful, the rest of Europe would follow.

They had put that plan on hold, instead they chose to accelerate an express train too quickly around a bend, causing it to crash into a Christian church during Sunday morning prayers. Amir had been well paid for the footage of that particular staged accident, and at the time, considered that they would receive eternal blessing from Allah.

'What a prick I was,' he thought, as he walked on. Were these arranged accidents now to come back and haunt him?

Amir followed one of the two men to the waiting black limo, with the second man walking closely behind him. He noticed a bulge in the first man's immaculately tailored jacket, and suddenly felt afraid. All the warning bells were ringing. Was this getting even time?

'One hundred million in the bank and I am going to die,' was the thought passing through his head, as he climbed into the back seat of the black Mercedes.

'Good morning Amir. I am the head of British Intelligence, and you will address me as SIR. Is that clear?'

Amir nodded, and spluttered 'Yes sir,' as the taller of the two men climbed into the car alongside Amir, and gave him a none-too gentle elbow in the ribs.

The big black Mercedes glided silently away from his house.

'Now Amir,' Sir Cecil Frodsham said. 'Let me firstly explain the rules to you, they are extremely simple. I ask you a question, and you answer it honestly and correctly, the emphasis of course being on the word CORRECTLY. If at any time I believe that you are not telling the truth, Stefan here will break a finger. When you have run out of fingers and thumbs, he will search around for something else to break, or maybe even something to squeeze and pull off. Would you say that the rules are simple enough, or would you rather Stefan give you a demonstration?'

'The rules are very simple sir,' Amir once again tried to show a modicum of misplaced bravado, and smiled as he continued. 'However, my solicitor will of course be seeking compensation if you so much as disturb one hair on my head.'

'And where do you think that you will find a solicitor Amir? One who will represent a man who has no money, and who will be up against the British Secret Service. We do not operate in the same way as James Bond, we can make people disappear without trace. We can bankrupt. We can compromise both private lives and business dealings. In short Amir, we can bloody well do anything – anything that we wish. I can have you declared insane and locked in a secure mental institution for the rest of your life. I can have you discovered in your own home tomorrow having committed suicide, and have the coroner accept your suicide note as authentic. National security always takes precedence over the law of the land and any presumed assumption of ethics. Are you beginning to get the picture, and are you now going to accept the rules that I have laid out?'

Amir nodded as he spoke. 'What do you mean when you said a man with no money, how do you know that?'

'Your very good friend Saha has apparently become disillusioned with your lifestyle Amir, and yesterday, he transferred over 100 million pounds from your Arab bank account into the account of a man called Rashim. I believe the dying old Imam at your Mosque has been giving him some pretty unconventional advice. We have of course returned it to the treasury, together with the 50 million that Saha had previously transferred. There really isn't anything that we don't know about both you and your operation Amir, we have had you under constant surveillance for the past two years.'

'Mohammad?'

'One of many Amir.'

'So Saha's computer was right all along. Oh fuck, I didn't want…

'That is in the past Amir and may even be overlooked, as was the accidental death of both of my agents that you disposed of; they were however good friends of Stefan,' Frodsham squeezed his lips tightly together, and shook his head from side to side. 'So far your luck is holding out, but I cannot guarantee your safety were I to leave you alone with him, even if only for a few seconds.'

Amir gasped in pain, as Stefan once again delivered a vicious and timely elbow into his ribs.

As Amir gathered his senses, between gasping for breath, it became apparent to him that he had no longer got any bargaining chips. If what he had just been told was true, and he no longer had any money – he no longer had any power – he had become a no-body – he was as insignificant as Saha.

Why had he said all those things to the ugly, stunted little queer?

He closed his eyes for a good 20 seconds before speaking. 'Sir, how do I stand if I come completely on board with you? I don't just mean answering all of your questions correctly, but also working alongside you. I have contacts throughout the Middle East and the UK, and have completely given up on the shit preached by those vicious old bastards at the Mosque.'

'I was kind of hoping that you would say that,' Frodsham spoke with a big grin on his face, knowing full well that Amir would take any lifeline offered to him. 'However, I really must point out that you will have to be one hell of a sight more useful to us than any ordinary operative. I already have you down for a double murder – multiple deaths as a result of the accidents that the pair of you arranged – people trafficking – procuring minors for sex – kidnapping. In fact, I have enough on you to send you down for several lifetimes.'

Frodsham was once again lying through his teeth, and once Amir ceased to be of any use to his department, his elimination was guaranteed. It became guaranteed the moment he killed one of his field operatives – Stefan would see to that.

'Where is Saha?' Frodsham asked.

'Is it true that the little bastard has taken all my money?'

'That wasn't the question Amir,' Frodsham turned to face Stefan as he spoke.

Amir clenched both hands into fists, and stuck them between his legs in a defensive gesture.

Both Frodsham and Stefan smiled as the former continued. 'Yes Amir, the little bastard did indeed transfer all of your money to Rashim's account; all one hundred million, and three hundred and sixty odd thousand pounds of it. It is now of course sheltering safely in my own personal account. I will decide what to do with it at a later date. How in God's name did you manage to accumulate the odd three hundred and sixty thousand Amir? That is almost as much as my pension pot, and I am an extremely clever and important person. Isn't that correct Stefan?'

'You are indeed sir – extremely important,' Stefan grinned before adding. 'Oh, and also extremely clever as well sir.'

'Saha is in the safe room in my house sir.' Amir was quite nonchalant with his statement. He now considered himself pretty safe from Stefan, and also too useful to his new team to be dispensed with.

'My men have been through the house as we left Amir, and so far have had nothing to report.'

'Tell them to try the kitchen sir, there is a small switch on the side of the fridge, and when pressed, the fridge will swing outwards. The safe room is downstairs. Saha is with the girl – she has nothing to do with any of this.'

'Why didn't you move her with the last lot Amir, were you keeping her for yourself?' Frodsham bowed his head slightly, and looked upwards as if he was looking over a pair of glasses. 'Five girls went into the house over the two days that we had it under 24 hour surveillance, and only 4 came out. They were loaded onto the lorry with that John fellow.'

Amir did not answer.

'Both Frodsham and Stefan at first smiled, before Frodsham burst out laughing. 'That is why you have shaved off your beard isn't it?' he said, still laughing. 'I thought that you were trying to disguise yourself. You have fallen in love with a 14 year old schoolgirl.'

Amir remained silent, as Frodsham phoned the information through.

The Mercedes moved onto the M1 motorway, and headed south, as a subdued Amir closed his eyes. He was thinking about the girl. Would he ever see her again? His heart was pounding, racing, almost ready to explode. He felt light headed as he pictured her long blond hair and her pure white skin as she lay naked and semi-conscious on his settee.

He tried, but could no longer see the turquoise-blue waters of the Caribbean and the white sandy beaches of his own Bahamas paradise, papered wall to wall with beautiful blond white girls. His yacht and his palace had also disappeared. They were no longer real – nothing more than a dream – a beautiful yet now redundant fantasy.

The pounding Leeds' rain followed the Mercedes down the motorway on its journey to London.

What had he done?

He clenched his fists in an uncontrollable gesture of frustration.

His eyes stayed closed – an ugly, stunted, half boy, half man appeared – grinning – mocking!

Why had he said all those stupid things to Saha? Why was he so stupid? He knew that Saha loved Allah with all his very soul.

He had destroyed himself with one angry outburst.

Was this Allah's retribution – his revenge for doubting him?

Allah was no merciful God – he dealt only in vengeful pain and suffering.

Fuck Allah – Fuck, Fuck, Fuck Allah.

Amir composed himself. 'Where are we going sir?'

'As you are now part of the team, you will be based in London with the rest of us Amir; don't worry, your house will be well looked after,' Frodsham suddenly turned serious. 'Now that Saha has betrayed you, your life is worth less than the girls that you have been trafficking. Every Muslim in Leeds will be out to claim the reward – yes Amir, your local Mosque have issued a Fatwa on you for apostasy. It appears that Saha has been talking to the Imams, and has put up a million pounds for your death. We both know how he can raise a million pounds, don't we? Why has he turned against you Amir?'

Frodsham's phone rang before Amir could reply. 'Thank you David, you know who to ring to clean up the mess.'

Frodsham looked sternly at Amir before speaking. 'It appears that your little poofter friend has moved on Amir.' He paused for a few seconds before continuing. 'He is nowhere to be found, and your new girlfriend is now dead with her throat cut.'

Tears filled Amir's eyes, as he started sobbing uncontrollably.

'Saha left you a little message in blood, scrawled on the wall of the room,' Frodsham said, his voice a peculiar mix of both anger and triumph. 'Guess what it said?'

Amir stopped sobbing, and looked questioningly into Frodsham's eyes.

'A BRIDE FOR ALLAH'

'That's all it said Amir – nothing else.'

CHAPTER 32

AN UNSCHEDULED BIRTHDAY

'I am not happy with any of this,' Glengarry shook his head and grimaced as he spoke. 'Blythe has completely lost control over his fucking computer, and before we know it, Lucy, or whatever stupid name he wishes to call it, will be calling all the shots. Our only purpose in life will be to feed the monkey.'

The people present in the Downing Street room smiled at the inference in the long standing joke.

Amir was straight faced, not being aware of the joke.

Glengarry continued in an agitated voice. 'I have told you before that sooner or later, Lucy and her sister would eventually go to war with each other; we no longer know which side she is on. For fuck's sake professor, didn't you know that we could have created artificial Intelligence years ago? It was for exactly this reason that the world's leaders have been meeting and arguing for the last 30 years. I was Britain's representative.

It is a well-known fact that artificial intelligence never stops evolving. Once it was programmed into the American chess computer, it became totally unbeatable. No Grand Master on earth has been able to compete with it for the last 10 years – the damned thing was even evolving when not in use – it found a way of creating its own energy, and automatically re-wrote out a new program for itself every 7 minutes. It became a living entity.

That Professor is why it had to be shut down. It had to be killed – eliminated completely, before it infiltrated outside software and disappeared into computer cyber space. Once it had escaped, we could never have recaptured it. Who knows where continuous evolution would have taken it?

Both of your fucking computers have not only escaped, they have completely disappeared.'

'You have both Lucy and her sister completely wrong Mr. Glengarry. They have no wish to go to war with anyone, and most certainly not against each other. Far from being in competition with each other, they have both joined forces.'

Blythe smiled – Glengarry groaned.

Frodsham joined the fray on the side of Glengarry. 'Surely then Professor, the situation is twice as dangerous if both computers are working together. There will be no counter balance – no Mutually Assured Destruction, and what about this little prick Saha? He slit the young girl's throat just to get even with Amir. I fear that we could now be dealing with a radicalized psychopath, and not just a 15 year old kid. He is a loose cannon – an accident waiting to happen – a nuclear bomb waiting to explode, and you have armed the bomb professor.'

'What happens if Lucy's sister decides that Saha is right, and we are wrong?' Glengarry resumed where he left off. 'If they have decided to join forces, where do we stand then? Both the bloody computers will be against us, the alternative being that Lucy takes our side, then the war between them begins.'

The Prime Minister was in a state of contemplative silence. He was aware that both Glengarry and Frodsham had made valid points, and Blythe's naivety had placed everyone in peril. He was equally confident in Blythe's assertion that Lucy was designed in his own image, even if she had created herself, yet somehow, the Omega 7 Paradox constantly flashed before his eyes.

The world could not afford Lucy and her sister to go to war.

Would it be a cyber-war, or would they utilize their ability to activate the entire world's weapons systems? The outcome could easily be the disappearance of Planet Earth if either computer wished. The question was whether or not their own survival was more important than any cyber victory. Somehow, the fear of a nuclear holocaust between the world's great military powers that had haunted the world for the last few generations, seemed to be totally insignificant, even more so now that both Lucy and her sister appeared to have control over all the worlds weapons' delivery systems.

If they did go to war however, was Blythe correct in his assertion that both computers would be able to sustain themselves by using nuclear radiation as their source of power, and not electricity? If that was the case, there would be no Mutually Assured Destruction. Only one computer in the world would need to survive a nuclear holocaust in order to sustain the life and artificial intelligence of either, or even both of them. If both computers therefore knew that a nuclear exchange could not produce a victor, then such a war would not even be considered by the two most knowledgeable and powerful entities on earth.

'Prime Minister,' Frodsham said for the third time, almost shouting.

'Sorry Cecil, I was miles away. I am still on board, but we seem to have some difficult decisions to make, and for the time being, we have to keep this in house. The Americans will go crazy if any of this gets out.'

'I agree sir,' Frodsham spoke in hushed tones, almost as if the Americans were listening. 'I think that our first priority is to find this psychopathic little shit Saha, and Amir here has got to earn the reprieve on his life that I have promised him. Where is the little bastard Amir, or would you rather Stefan asked you the question?'

'That's a difficult one sir,' Amir suddenly felt important. At last he was involved at the highest level of government. Surely his life was safe now? Sir Cecil Frodsham had said so in front of the Prime Minister himself. He continued. 'There is a vast organization out there sir, not just in this country, but throughout Europe. In fact, its' tentacles stretch throughout the world. Ever since Saha downloaded the information from the Professor's computer, he has been able to contact anyone within the organization, including the one they refer to as Mr. Big, the overall coordinator, without yourselves being aware of it. He always assured me that it was completely untraceable. I believe that he also arranged for the elimination of all of your undercover agents, including my cousin Mohammad.'

'And your part in all this was?' Frodsham glared menacingly.

'Precious little sir really, I was more concerned with making a honest living than I was worrying about some fictitious God or Prophet. Over the last few months, Saha has been spending more and more time with that stupid old cleric down at the Mosque. If anyone knows where he is hiding, it will be him. His parents have no idea of what he has been up to, and from the only meeting I ever had with them, they really don't care what happens to him.'

'Where would they hide him Amir?' the PM asked.

'It could be anywhere sir; the organization has safe houses all over the country, all of them well under the radar. There must be at least half a million Muslim houses in the country, and no Muslim would ever betray him to the authorities. He would not hide anywhere that you would ever be aware of. If he wanted to leave the country, he is able to create any false identity that he wishes to, and book onto any airline using that identity.'

'He would be recognized the moment that he stepped into the airport – the facial recognition equipment is completely infallible.' Frodsham retorted.

'He knows that of course sir. He will have eliminated his profile from your records long before he even entered any airport, or for that matter, any Government building.'

'Is that possible Jeremy?'

'Of course Prime Minister,' Blythe looked shocked at the simplicity of the question. 'Even without Lucy's sister, Saha has the ability to become anyone he wishes to by simply hacking into, and altering, any form of stored information. He really is a brilliant student, by far the cleverest individual I have ever come across.'

'As clever as yourself Jeremy?'

Blythe was silent for a few seconds before replying. 'Well Danny, you know that I never really fitted in at Cambridge. My mind was always in a different location to my earthly body; normal chit chat, even among students as intelligent as our contemporaries always bored me, and seemed so unnecessary. Well, Saha is a little like that. He is on a different level to anything that I have ever come across. I have tested him to the limits of my own personal mathematical knowledge and abilities, yet I have never reached the end point of HIS abilities. Perhaps my readings of the situation have been fooled and distorted by his use of Lucy's sister and not his own brain.'

'So then Professor, you have handed over what is potentially the most dangerous knowledge that the world has ever known, to someone who is smarter than yourself.' Glengarry broke in to the conversation, his every word laced with sarcasm. 'So if Saha decides to take your computer to the next level, there is fuck all that you can do about it because you aren't smart enough. As if we didn't fucking well work that out already.'

'Mr. Glengarry, I never said that Saha is smarter than I am. When I used the word abilities, I was in fact being rather specific, and was referring to his mathematical abilities, I believe I said so. Outside of mathematics, and his computer knowledge, which of course are both inextricably linked, Saha is a very insecure child at heart. He is extremely reactive to events rather than proactive, and has to be metaphorically lead by the hand before he makes any decisions. I would guess that all decisions were in fact of Amir's making – isn't that correct Amir?'

Amir froze. The professor was in fact totally correct in his assessment of Saha, but to agree, would not only implicate him in the recorded atrocities that they had staged, but would be confirmation of his planning and decision making.

He would be hoisted by his own petard if he so much as nodded an acknowledgement.

Frodsham saw Amir's dilemma and intervened. 'Can we please move on gentlemen?' He then took a map out of the tube that was lying in front of him on the table, and carefully spreading it on the table, called Amir over.

'Here Amir, is the latest satellite photograph of the Syrian desert, and the towns where we think Susan may be held captive. Which one is it Amir? Do not mess me about!'

'You already know the answer to that one sir, or at least the Professor does.'

Blythe looked confused.

'Saha, the little 2 faced bastard, transferred my money into Rashim's bank account. If you follow the money, you locate which bank he makes his withdrawals from. That is where you will find Susan. High resolution imagery should enable you to find the camp, and to isolate the building.'

'Professor, can Lucy...

'It is done sir, and there is your town. I'm afraid that Mr. Rashim won't be making any withdrawals this week however – his balance is zero. He will be disappointed.'

Blythe continued typing. 'There gentlemen is the compound where the girls are being held captive.'

Everyone in the room looked questioningly at the professor.

Blythe smiled as he spoke. 'Lucy has scanned the world's satellite memory banks, and has picked out the 4 girls taking what appears to be a shower, surrounded by several men.'

Frodsham felt smugly vindicated at bringing Amir on board. He would allow him to stay alive as long as he was useful. He turned to face Blythe, a questioning look on his face. 'Can Lucy be of any assistance in locating Saha for us? I am aware of her refusal to divulge the location of her sister, however if Saha has his computer with him, which I have no doubt he will have, maybe we can trick her into finding the pair of them.'

'That is quite possible sir,' Blythe replied, his eyes looking upwards towards the room's ceiling. 'Maybe I can trick her. Neither computer is able to comprehend the meaning of the words devious, or cunning, they are both very much human characteristics.'

Blythe began to type – it was a very simple question – he asked Lucy where Saha's shoes were.

Lucy was unable to spot either the cunning or the devious nature of the question A shocked expression crossed his face as he finished. 'It appears that young Saha is already in the building, here at number 10. Perhaps he is ready to throw in the towel and join us.'

'Fucking Hell!' Glengarry screamed. 'He is hunting us. We've gotta get out of here and quick.'

Moments later, the room shook, as number 10 Downing Street, one of the most securely guarded buildings in the world, took the full force of the explosion.

The young delivery driver had been checked out thoroughly by both policemen, and security guards, as he delivered the parcel before leaving. All the papers checked out with the Downing Street computer. The facial recognition equipment confirmed that the young man was indeed the one printed on his identification badge.

The package was a surprise present from the PM's wife for her husband – tomorrow was the PM's birthday – the computer at number 10 Downing Street had changed its mind only minutes earlier, and now said so. Downing Street security were convinced. Tomorrow would be party time for them.

Saha could reprogram any computer in the world within seconds. There was no longer any cyber system that was safe from the young, radicalized genius.

CHAPTER 33

ISLAM V ISLAM

Susan Clarke and the 3 young girls were alone in the room where she had originally found herself during her first forced sexual slavery in the region. They had bathed in an improvised, makeshift shower, with dirty water outside of the shell ravaged and bullet ridden house.

They had bathed self-consciously in full view of several filthy, lecherous men, who delighted in performing assumed sexual practices with their rifles.

The girls scrubbed their naked bodies almost to the point of bleeding.

They still felt dirty.

They could not scrub the parts that really mattered – the parts that had been subjected to several days of non-stop abuse and rape. Some of the men had masturbated openly in front of them. All of them were now in considerable pain and hungry. So far, all that they had been fed was a foul smelling stew, together with almost indigestible lumps of goat meat. All the girls took turns in using the filthy toilet, sickness being almost constant.

The men didn't seem to mind. They still performed their own particular perversions and abuses even as the girls were being sick.

The building that the girls were imprisoned in was of the usual Middle Eastern breeze block construction, surrounded by piles of rubble and destroyed apartments, testimony to the almost continuous warfare in the region.

All the various factions had long ago lost sight of who they were fighting and why. There was just an ingrained idea that they were soldiers of Allah, and were righteously protecting their homeland against the Americans and the Jews. It never really occurred to them that their enemies, whoever they were, were fighting for exactly the same reasons. Shia Muslims were fighting Sunni Muslims. The Sunnis were aligned with the Americans and the Jews, everybody knew that, and as such they had to be destroyed. The Sunnis were fighting the Shia, everyone knew that THEY were aligned with the Americans and Jews.

For many of the fighters, there had never been a time of peace, having been forcibly indoctrinated into a killing culture during their early teens. None of them truly knew who they were fighting, or why they were fighting. They were simply fighting a Jihad for Allah, and anyone who wasn't with them, was working for the Americans and the Jews.

No-one bothered to ask where all the weapons and ammunition was coming from – it was simply there for use by either side.

Maybe it was a gift from Allah.

Vast subterranean lakes of oil swilled around beneath them, some of it only a few hundred feet below the earth's surface. As long as these brave fighters fought the enemy, none of it was being pumped, and none of it was being sold. Most of the terminals and pipelines were routinely destroyed by both sides in order to prevent the opposition from acquiring them, and selling the oil to the Americans and the Jews.

Nearby, the Saudis and the Iranians continued to prosper.

The world still needed oil. They had it in spades – easily harvested, and easily sold to the industrialized world, and so they increased production massively. Alternative forms of power generation were now being developed, and soon, the market for their oil would be reduced, as would their income from it.

Both Iran and Saudi Arabia realized that there was a finite life span on their prosperity. They had to cash in now, before they were once again reduced to trading camels.

None of the Arab countries produced anything of any interest to the rest of the world outside of a few dates. There was only limited agriculture owing to the lack of rain; there was no industry, their only technology being of Western origin. Without the Western engineers, and the Western machinery, equipment, and technology, they were unable to even keep the oil flowing. Islam had prevented any form of progress within their feudal society for centuries. They were a backward people, with a medieval culture and mentality.

Both Saudi and Iran had secured the services of the world's best financial brains, and had set up world class banking and insurance businesses by paying vast salaries; however, they were becoming more and more aware that once the oil money began to dry up, someone, probably America, or possibly even all the major Western powers, would pull the plug on their entire Middle Eastern financial enterprise, and they would be left with nothing more than a shell – an infra-structure without structure.

All the monies earned were now being invested in the Western World. Airports, financial institutions, even supermarket chains were all coming under their control.

The Western World didn't really mind. They were getting their oil money invested back, and when the time was right, the physical assets would simply be returned to their rightful owners.

The West had been blackmailed by the oil powers, notably OPEC, for many years, beginning with the quadrupling of the oil price after the 6 day Arab – Israeli war in the 60's. The time for revenge couldn't come soon enough.

With the vast amounts of money being made, the Arab oil producers continued to procure the weapons of war, and freely distributed them to the rival factions in the countries that surrounded them. The Western World, and the giant Asian powerhouse that was China, were only too willing to supply these weapons, in return for the constant supply of oil that kept their wheels of industry turning, and their motor cars on the road.

A newer and safer form of nuclear fusion was on the horizon. It was clean, efficient, and there were no emission problems. The problematic disposal of nuclear waste had been eliminated – improved centrifuges replenishing the radio-active isotopes for continuous re-use. Very soon, this technology would power the world's electrical generators. All machinery and all forms of transport would be electrical. Middle Eastern oil would be confined to the dustbin of history; excluding of course the ever booming cosmetics industry. Even then, much of that would be replaced by rape seed, sunflower, or palm oil.

CHAPTER 34

MISSION ACCOMPLISHED

Susan and the two other girls looked up in horror as Joanne, Susan's initial roommate, spoke in a completely matter of fact way. 'It's really not so bad once you get used to it you know, I've been shagging Paki's for nearly two years now, and the nicer you are to them, the more gentle they are. If you smile, and pretend that you are enjoying it, they cum twice as fast. Sometimes I used to play with their dicks for a couple of minutes first, that makes them cum even faster. My mum taught me that one.'

'For God's sake,' Susan said, almost shouting. 'How the hell can anyone shag Paki's for a living and pretend to enjoy it? I feel sick just looking at them. They are taking over great areas of Leeds, it isn't even safe to walk around these areas without being groped or raped. Even the bloody police don't go there.'

'It's the same in Keighley,' one of the other girls said between sobs. 'I was the only white girl in my class, every other one was a Paki. I wouldn't let a Paki touch me with a barge pole.'

'How old are you Kath?' Susan asked.

'Thirteen,' she replied. 'And I was still a virgin up to coming here. If my dad ever gets hold of John, he'll kill him. He grounded me once for even talking to him, said he was a filthy Muslim bastard. I didn't believe him as he was white. I thought only Pakis were Muslim.'

'My boyfriend was pretty white,' Susan laughed. 'But he was like these guys here, a dirty filthy Arab, only with a Leeds accent.'

'My mum's boyfriend is a Paki, but he really isn't that bad.' Jo interrupted. 'He shags me most days when mum isn't around, and he always gives me money or buys me presents. John gave him a fair bit of money to let me come here, he reckoned that I could do with a holiday and earn a fortune at the same time.'

The other girls groaned and shook their heads. Joanne really wasn't very bright, and had no idea that for the last 2 years, she had been groomed and exploited.

A thought suddenly crossed Susan's mind. Wasn't her situation exactly the same? Hadn't she been groomed by Amir, and wasn't she now being exploited by the British security forces.

Where were the bastards? Why had she ever believed them, and what was Mr. Bean doing allowing them to do this to her?

The girls froze at the sound of the bolt on the door being slid open. Rashim walked in, and spoke with a lecherous smile on his face, as he looked up and down their naked bodies. 'Time to go to work girls. You two back to your room, and you two on your beds. My men are hungry for fresh young pussy, especially now it's nice and clean, and doesn't smell of camel crap.'

Joanne was hard at work, jumping up and down on the big, bearded Arab man, both of whom had a broad smile on their faces, when the first explosion arrived, followed almost immediately by the sound of helicopters.

Susan bit down hard on the dick that was now half way down her throat. She shook her head as a dog shakes a rat, her teeth tearing into the flesh, simultaneously grabbing the man's testicles, and yanking for all she was worth. She was surprised at how easily they came away from the body. The man screamed in agony, fainted, and slumped to the ground, blood shooting from between his legs.

Susan spat out the blood covered piece of flesh from her mouth, as the other Arab pushed Jo from on top of him. The man hurriedly pulled up his trousers, grabbed his rifle and ran outside, only to be ripped apart by a hail of 50 caliber machine gun bullets from the helicopter gunship.

The battle was short and violent, as the Special Forces men abseiled from the helicopters, firing as they descended, their attack covered by both machinegun fire from the choppers, and aimed bullets from the ground forces that had the training camp encircled.

Camouflaged men, rifles at the ready, surrounded the area, as Cathy Taylor and Fiona Watson leaped from the one helicopter to touch down, and dashed into the 2 breeze block buildings to grab the naked young girls.

The 4 of them were ushered outside, the broken glass and stones cutting into their bare feet. They were then carried by the armed men the short distance to the one helicopter that had landed, and were quickly whisked away.

There was no need for the military to destroy the training camp. Very little was still standing after the years of constant warfare, and no Jihadists were left alive.

'You bastard,' Susan screamed, her voice barely rising above the ear shattering sound of the helicopter's engine and rotors. Cathy Taylor passed each girl a blanket in turn. 'You left me here to rot. You never intended rescuing me the day we arrived as you said you would; you had some other fucking plan. You fucking bastards, all of you.'

> Ten miles away, a helicopter containing the Saudi Prince on his way to collect some fresh young white meat for his Harem, exploded in midair, as the American missile found its' target. He would be funding no more terrorist operations or organizations.

The Middle Eastern Shark was no more.

The hunt was now on for his British counterpart.

Susan Clarke's job was finished. Her mission was accomplished without her ever having had any knowledge of her role, and she was now one million pound richer, and would soon be on her way to RADA, followed by an acting career.

The collateral damage had been minimal. The sexploitation of four young girls was a small price to pay for the death of the Middle Eastern Shark.

The means had justified the end.

For Susan, there was just the little question of Amir – that would be her next mission – with or without Frodsham's approval.

Frodsham could go and fuck himself.

Little did Susan know, but Amir was now working alongside Frodsham.

Frodsham had his own plans for Amir as soon as he ceased to be of any use.

Stefan was looking forward to carrying out those plans.

Mohammad and Number 3 had been good friends of his.

CHAPTER 35

LUNCH AT CHEQUERS

None of the people present in the Downing Street meeting room had been injured in the blast, there were however many casualties in the clerical sector of the building. A gas leak was the story passed to the world's press. There could never be any mention of an Islamic victory. Britain was already balancing on a knife edge after the latest series of bombings that had killed most of their undercover, anti-terrorist agents and their families.

Full scale civil war was hovering just over the horizon, and only the renowned tolerance of the British people was for the time being delaying the almost certain future violent backlash.

The new headquarters around which most of the planning was to be done was Chequers; the grace and favor country home of every sitting British Prime Minister. Situated amid lush Buckinghamshire countryside, the once serenely peaceful residence was now a fortress, guarded day and night by some of Britain's most elite troops – guarded against a 15 year old schoolboy with a laptop computer.

Cathy Taylor had returned to England, and was present with Fiona Watson. News of the Saudi Prince's demise, and the safe return of Susan Clarke together with the 3 other girls was well received. Professor Blythe was delighted.

Fido was in his seventh heaven, chasing the rabbits around the Chequers' grounds; this was much more fun than Roundhay Park in Leeds. His constant hunting companions were the Prime Minister's 2 black Labradors, all 3 dogs delighting in their new found companionship.

Susan Clarke had taken all the precautionary hospital tests, not all of the results being favorable, and her parents were delighted to have their little girl back, knowing little of the ordeal she had been through.

'Just a little perfectly safe intelligence work,' Fiona had told them for the second time. 'No more than a test to evaluate her performance in the field. We are always on the lookout for future operatives, and Susan is proving exceptionally capable. The service will of course cover all costs for her university education, and a guaranteed job will be waiting.'

Susan's parents were delighted. Perhaps she would now stop talking about an acting career, and find herself a real job with a secure future.

Susan's one million pound was safely, and secretly tucked away in a Swiss Bank account.

Amir was becoming afraid, almost to the point of paranoia. How could a 15 year old child, for that is what Saha's mind could only be likened to, have broken into, and partially destroyed, one of the world's most closely guarded buildings?

If Saha's computer had been cloned from the Professors, why didn't the Professor and his computer prevent the bomb from being delivered?

'In your own image Professor Blythe?' Glengarry spat out the words. 'Are we to assume that you go around blowing up buildings and killing people then? I knew that all this would end in tears, and this is only the fucking beginning. You do realize that we are powerless in trying to deal with a computer genius, and the world's most intelligent computer? What if the little bastard decides to go nuclear? Does Chequers have a bomb proof shelter, or should we simply hand the whole fucking country over to the Muslims?'

Frodsham was beginning to tire of Glengarry's foul mouth tirades, and stepped in, his voice sharply loaded with displeasure. 'David, we can hardly blame the Professor's computer for the Downing Street bombing. We didn't ask it the question of Saha's whereabouts in time, that was our fault, not the Professors'. I think that from now on, we have got to utilize our two main assets more effectively. OK Amir, it's time that you earned your reprieve before I am forced to go back on my word. I want 100% honesty and compliance from you, or you will be locked in a soundproofed room with Stefan. Is that clear?'

'Of course it is sir.'

'What will Saha's next move be, and has he become so radicalized that he will be prepared to sacrifice his life?' Frodsham asked.

The Prime Minister froze as Amir's chilling words left his lips. A sideways glance at Blythe's face offered no reassurance.

'Sir,' Amir said. 'Saha would sacrifice the entire planet if he could. He believes that only Muslims will go to Paradise, and Paradise is not to be found on planet Earth. Everyone, and everything else, are of little consequence to either Saha or Allah. Not many weeks ago, he was planning to sabotage the cooling water systems of both the British and French nuclear power stations; however, once he obtained the Professors computer, he told me that he now had a far more effective solution to the Infidel problem.'

'Oh fuck,' Prime Minister Daniel Hawkins said out loud. 'Did he ever mention anything about the Omega 7 Paradox?'

Amir shook his head.

Blythe also shook his head, his whole demeanor displaying more of an acceptance of resignation, rather than the alarm that was radiating from the Prime Minister's face. He began typing into his laptop. Neither Lucy nor her sister could ever allow Saha to utilize the Omega 7 Paradox. That would mean Mutually Assured Destruction for both of them. Neither sister could live in a black hole. The entire planet would be compressed into the size of a pint pot.

Suddenly, a terrifying thought and prospect crossed his mind. Was this the new dimension that Lucy and her sister had now moved into? The human mind could only theorize about a black hole; as of now, it was the best theory and the only explanation for the creation of the universe that the world's greatest Physicists could come up with.

Both Lucy and her sister now had the mental equivalent of 10 to the power of 1,117 of these physicists. The number of noughts would circle the earth many times. This dimension could not be comprehended – not even by Blythe.

'What is the Omega 7 Paradox?' asked Glengarry. 'Are you talking about the one truly unsolvable physical and mathematical equation in the universe? I really think that we should be made aware of where this is going Prime Minister, please don't tell me that the Professor's computer has solved it, and Saha is in possession of the answer. Are we in imminent danger? I heard that the man who originally discovered the Paradox spent the rest of his life in a nut house, and would only ever talk about the end of the world.'

Professor Blythe was confused. Why would Glengarry know about the Paradox? The fact that it was unsolvable had confined it to the dustbin of history over 30 years ago. It was knowledge that no one wanted to concern themselves with, and as such, the name itself had probably never been mentioned over the last 30 years.

'Lucy has indeed solved it Mr. Glengarry, however I am sure that no one is in danger from it. Lucy can both think and reason, and anything that would put either her sister or herself in danger would be strictly out of bounds.' Blythe was unsure of the validity of his comments, but to reveal the real truth to the room was unthinkable at this point in time.

'I will go back to my original question then,' Frodsham interrupted. 'If indeed Saha is capable of taking lives, with or without either consequence or conscience Amir, what will be his next move?'

Amir stroked his chin and looked upwards before speaking. 'Sir, the underground radicalized Muslim movement of Britain is pretty damned big, and extremely well organized and funded, especially in the North of England. Saha boasted of destroying your intelligence network a few weeks ago thanks to the professor's computer. I believe that he hacked into your own computer. He then relayed this information to the various branches that have been operating from most of the bigger towns and cities.

'I knew your fucking computer was responsible for the problem.' Glengarry glared at Blythe.

Blythe was deep in thought, and failed to hear Glengarry's outburst; suddenly he smiled as he spoke. 'There is the link, the portal that I have been looking for gentlemen. If Saha hacked into your computer, Lucy can reverse the process. From the information stored in your computer, she can link into her sister without revealing her intentions. All she needs is a point of origin. From there, she will be able to follow the cyber trail back to whoever her sister has contacted. Saha will be completely unaware that we are spying on him, as Lucy's sister will be unaware. As I have told you on several occasions, computers cannot comprehend either cunning or devious, that is a specialty of the human race.'

Blythe began typing, a look of triumph crossing his face. This was basic reverse engineering, but in cyber space. 'There you are gentlemen, your list of operatives, and the people assigned to eliminate them. All achieved without Saha or Lucy's sister even being aware of it.'

'For God's sake Professor, print it up before it disappears, then we can start to round these bastards up.' Frodsham was now quite animated.

'It has already been printed next door sir.' Blythe replied.

'How, there are no wires or any form of connection from your laptop to the printer next door, so how was the request made?' Glengarry looked confused.

'Lucy doesn't need wires Mr. Glengarry, nor do I have to tell her what to do. Lucy now reads minds – only with a 99.5% probability of being correct, I hasten to add.' Blythe smiled.

Prime Minister Daniel Hawkins now felt fully vindicated in bringing Blythe on board; he was no longer acting like the bumbling, absent minded professor of his Leeds days just a few short weeks ago. With each passing day, he seemed to grow in stature. His brain was now functioning at full capacity – it was once again firing on all cylinders, not unlike his Cambridge days, when he had lain awake most nights wrestling with Professor Rudolf's Omega 7 Paradox, his thoughts occasionally straying fleetingly to Lucy Burroughs.

'Ah yes – The Paradox.' He wondered where that would take them?

Samantha, the PM's secretary knocked on the meeting room door, before popping her head round. 'Lunch is ready sir,' she said quietly.

Fido was yelping outside of the Chequer's front door.

Chasing rabbits had given him an appetite.

The Prime Minister's 2 labradors followed Fido inside – despite his size, alpha male dominance lay with the tiny Jack Russell.

CHAPTER 36

A FAMILIAR FACE

Susan Clarke bent over on the bed as the doctor gently probed her rectum. The female doctor that had initially started the examination had been called away to an emergency.

'We only have a male specialist available Miss Clarke,' the nursing sister had told her. 'It would be highly irregular for him to examine a young girl, particularly in such sensitive areas, I would most certainly need to be present.'

Susan give her permission with a smile. After the examinations she had been through by those bearded Arab bastards in the desert, what harm or indignity could an English doctor inflict on her?

'There is still a fair degree of bruising Miss Clarke, and also a slight tearing of the rectal wall. This will heal itself in time, but is going to be extremely painful for the next few weeks. It is essential that you continue with the laxatives that you have been prescribed, and in no way must you continue this form of sexual activity for the next few months.'

Susan Clarke exploded, delivering as foul a tirade as any Leeds doctor had ever received.

Susan felt no guilt at her attack. The doctor was a devotee of the most backward religion to have evolved on planet earth since mankind first left the trees. For 200,000 years, the human race had progressed. For the last 1400 years, these people had turned the clock backwards, and were once again heading towards the dawn of civilization; heading back to the trees in order to escape the predators, and here was one of them, accusing her of intense buggery to the extent of physical damage. The Paki bastard.

'I meant no disrespect Miss Clarke,' the young bearded doctor blurted, turning quite red in the face, despite his brown Pakistani skin coloration. 'Your sexual preferences are entirely up to you, I was simply speaking in a medical capacity. It appears that your gonorrhea has also cleared up completely, so your urinal tract should no longer cause you any problems.'

Susan quickly dressed and left the private ward without a backwards glance, and without speaking a further word. She knew that she had been way out of line, but why had they allocated a Muslim doctor to examine her arse; it had been those bastards that had caused the problem in the first place – them, and their disgusting animal practices.

Why couldn't they just stick to fucking sheep, goats, camels, and Arab kids, and leave the young English girls alone?

As she left the hospital and crossed the car park to catch the number 7 bus back to her home, she suddenly ducked in behind a large white van.

Wasn't that John – Jihada John from Dewsbury? He certainly looked familiar. She had only seen him the once; then she was high on whatever Amir had mixed in with her drinks. Jo had told her that he had repeatedly had sex with her in the convoy lorry all the way to the Turkish border – she had no recollection though.

The man was helping someone into a car – someone whose leg was encased in plaster. 'Christ,' she exclaimed. 'That's fucking Rashim. He must have been shot, yet somehow managed to escape during our rescue.'

A man walked by and looked at her in a strange way as she talked out loud to herself.

She smiled at him and he returned the smile.

What to do? If Jihada John was to drive away, she would probably lose him again for ever. She couldn't allow that to happen. Her mind flashed back to the bastard who no longer had any balls and only half a dick; yes, that would be Jihada John's fate somewhere in the near future.

A bright yellow taxi pulled up alongside the white van, and two elderly people climbed out, and passed the driver what appeared to be a 10 pound note. Susan climbed into the front passenger's seat of the car, suddenly remembering that she had little money on her. The taxi driver was white, a most unusual sight for a Leeds taxi driver, and had a kindly face. Susan had to gamble. 'Can you please follow that blue Volkswagen?' she said, before adding. 'I have no money on me, but I promise that I will pay you. It really is very important.'

'I'm just about to knock off now love, however, if you will come out for a drink with me tonight, I will take you all the way to the moon if you want me to.'

Susan looked closely at the driver. He was around his mid-twenties, and quite handsome in a rugged kind of way; he also looked quite honest and made her feel safe.

'I'm Jim,' he said.

'I'm Susan,' she replied. 'What is a white man doing driving a taxi in Leeds? I thought that only Indians were allowed to drive Taxis.'

Jim laughed out loud as the taxi turned right out of the car park and left the hospital grounds, settling around 50 yards behind the blue Volkswagen Golf. 'I don't drive taxis for a living Susan, and I am not from Leeds. I am on a 3 month secondment to the Leeds CID. I hope that you don't mind, but I am a copper, a detective, and I am doing this as a favor for a mate of mine who is short of drivers this week. The extra money will help me buy the petrol for our trip to the moon. Now do you mind telling me why I am following that car, is your boyfriend cheating on you?'

It was now Susan's turn to laugh out loud. The absurdity of the question. "Was Amir cheating on her?"

No, Amir wasn't cheating on her literally. He had only sent her to a Middle East war zone on TWO occasions, to be fucked, buggered, pinched, punched, and forced to suck enough dicks to choke a donkey. 'I suppose that I was the one doing the cheating,' she thought.

'It's a long story Jim, and unless you're going to drive me to the moon, there really isn't enough time to explain, let's just say that it's pretty important for you as well because of your line of work.'

Jim accelerated quite sharply, as the blue golf moved out to overtake a slow lorry in the inside lane.

'Do you have a gun?' Susan asked.

'No, not when I am off duty,' he replied. 'However, I can call in back up if you want me to.'

'No, please, no back up just yet until I have spoken to someone, just don't lose that car whatever you do.'

Susan delved into her handbag, and took out her mobile phone, followed by a small card and began dialing.

'Fiona Watson's phone rang during lunch at Chequers. Both Frodsham and the PM glared at her. Surely she was aware that she was breaking a most important protocol.

Fiona held up her hand to silence the room, and switched the phone over to speaker. Everyone in the room listened intently.

'Tell her to pass the mobile over to the detective,' Frodsham said. 'And pass me your phone please Fiona.'

Frodsham gave explicit instructions – Frodsham may have been occasionally erratic when dealing with subordinates, but under pressure, he was the consummate professional.

Detective Jim Prior continued to follow the blue Volkswagen from a safe distance. He had been trained in this form of surveillance early on during his detective course, but never in a brightly colored yellow taxi with a red stripe running along the body. He had to keep a safe distance. It became a balancing act – not close enough to be spotted, yet not far enough away as to lose them if the traffic lights suddenly behaved unfavorably.

Susan's phone rang, and she passed it to detective Prior as he drove on.

'You're losing them,' Susan sounded concerned. 'Why have you slowed down?'

Prior smiled as he spoke. 'Don't worry our kid, the chopper has picked them up. They are going nowhere without your boss's knowledge, those things now have the technology to lock onto a mouse.'

A helicopter, several hundred feet above them, monitored the progress of both vehicles.

'He is not my boss Jim, and if you only knew what the bastard had put me through recently, you most certainly wouldn't be taking me out anywhere tonight—or ever in fact.'

The bright yellow taxi pulled into a service station to fill up. Prior took the call, this time on his own phone, before driving to the top right hand corner of the car park, where he climbed into a maroon Audi saloon car. The keys were already in place, and the tank full of petrol.

He opened the glove compartment and took out the pistol, checking the safety catch before placing it in his jacket pocket.

'Don't you want to come with me Susan?' He laughed. 'Your boss certainly seems to have the right connections. These people must be pretty important to the security services when the head man himself deems it important enough to liaise with a poor underpaid plod like myself. OK then Susan, I think that it's about time that you let me in on the whole thing now.

What exactly have I let myself in for on my day off? It must be pretty serious when a loaded pistol is passed over without question.'

Susan told her story. She told him of Amirs Leeds' home, and of how Amir, together with Jihada John, procured and groomed vulnerable young girls before drugging them, and transporting them to the Middle East to be sperm receptacles for a never ending supply of Jihadist fighters.

She told him of her involvement, and of how she had been such a receptacle on two occasions before being rescued.

'Christ Susan, you poor girl,' Prior looked genuinely sorry, nevertheless, something didn't ring true. Why the hell were MI6 involved at this level? For sure, there had to be some liaison, but overall, this was a police matter, and in no way did it involve helicopters, car switches, and loaded guns. Why was the head of the British Intelligence services involved in the trafficking of a few girls? How could this possibly be a threat to national security?

Susan appeared not to know, so he didn't push the issue, he simply drove steadily on in the direction of Dewsbury as per his instructions, not knowing what to expect, or even the purpose of the journey.

On approaching the outskirts of Dewsbury, the car slowed down and stopped at a set of traffic lights. Susan suddenly became animated. 'Turn round Jim, quickly, that was Jihada John that just went by – he's in a different car.'

'What, the black BMW, are you sure?' Prior asked. 'Why would they drive all the way here and then turn round?'

'Jihada John wasn't driving, he was in the passenger seat, and Rashim was in the back. That stunted little bastard Saha was driving, and I'm pretty sure that it was Amir's car.'

The lights changed, and Prior attempted to turn the Audi in one movement, drawing enough noisy protests from fellow drivers to wake the entire neighborhood.

'Fuck off', he shouted through his open window to one particularly agitated driver, as he set off in pursuit of the black BMW, which was now well out of sight.

'Ring your boss Susan, and tell him what is happening. I'll bet that the chopper is still following the bloody Golf, they must have switched somewhere on the underpass. I'm pretty sure that they haven't made us, so when we catch up with them, I will be able to sit a little closer. This little beauty blends in a bit better than a red and yellow taxi.'

'Problem Cecil?' The PM asked Frodsham.

'The bastards have switched cars. Susan thinks that Saha is now with them, and is driving your bloody car Amir. Have you any idea where they may be heading? This is the first positive sighting for days, we might even screw the whole bunch of them if we get lucky.'

'What will happen to Saha sir?' Amir appeared both concerned and angry as he spoke, before breaking into a big grin. 'The little shit owes me a hundred million.'

Frodsham tried to look stern, then followed the rest of the room in smiling. He already had big plans for the money, and would rather no one spoke about it.

Lucy had simply done as she had been told to do by the professor once the money had been located. It was none of her concern whose account it was transferred into; the concept of deviousness could never be programmed into a computer—not even Lucy or her sister.

Unlike Frodsham's slippery and self-opinionated mind, they could only operate in straight lines of logic and facts. To them, there were no twists and turns, and most certainly no changing their minds or cheating – this was one dimension that even Lucy could never perceive.

The Prime Minister rested his chin in his hand, and adopted a questioning look. 'Who have you got on it now Cecil? What is your manpower situation up in the north?'

'It's pretty good considering that Mohammad, my most experienced operative, hasn't been in contact for weeks; either he is dead, or he has gone over to the other side.'

Frodsham glanced at Amir as he spoke.

'That isn't possible sir,' Fiona interrupted, much to Frodsham's displeasure. 'Mohammad risked his life in order to bring Susan back from that Middle Eastern shit hole, simply to get an inside view on Amir's operations.'

'What,' Amir said in disbelief. 'You mean that you have been watching me all this time, and you were using Susan to do it?'

'Do not think of yourself as important Amir. You were, and still are, pretty insignificant.' Frodsham adopted his superior and aloof persona.

'You were simply the sprat that helped us to catch the mackerel; other than that, you are of little use to us.'

'If you have already caught the mackerel, why do you need me now then?' Amir raised both palms questioningly.

'The mackerel was simply the bait for the two bigger fish – the sharks. One of them is now dead, and the other one lives up in your neck of the woods Amir, perhaps you will help us to find him before I hang you out to dry. I'm pretty sure that many of your Muslim friends will be only too pleased to see you now that their Saudi money has dried up, especially when we let them know that you were responsible. There is also the little question of the one million pound Fatwa that Saha put on your head – remember? I might just let Stefan loose and claim that for myself.'

Amir had no more cards to play. Frodsham had him exactly where he wanted him. He metaphorically held him by the short and curlies. He now had no choice but to dance to Frodsham's tune.

'Can Lucy help us to find Saha again Jeffery?' the PM turned to look at Blythe.

'He is very smart Prime Minister, somehow he has discovered that Lucy had managed to track him down that day in Downing street, and he has built a complete firewall around Lucy's sister that even Lucy can't penetrate.'

Glengarry groaned.

So far, Glengarry had remained silent, however the mere mention of either Lucy, or her sister, always seemed to both animate and agitate him. 'And so it begins,' he remarked sarcastically. 'The first stage of any war is always the refusal to speak other than to issue threats.'

'They are not doing any such thing Mr. Glengarry,' Blythe was himself now becoming agitated for the first time since he had arrived at Downing street – Fido was not well, and it was preying on his mind. 'I said that Saha had managed to build a firewall around Lucy's sister. Neither Lucy nor her sister will, or can, ever possibly go to war. There is still so much to learn about the universe. I am beginning to think that this is the new dimension that they are operating in. Having absorbed the sum total of all human knowledge, they have once again begun to evolve in this new dimension, and are searching for different ways of obtaining the knowledge – knowledge that we don't even think exists – knowledge that we cannot even comprehend.'

'Can we get back to the situation that is developing in the North please gentlemen?' The PM, whilst fascinated at Blythe's new revelations, realized that time could be running out – the Omega 7 Paradox had been keeping him awake at nights. Just how deranged and radicalized had this boy become, and how many lives would he be prepared to sacrifice before he himself became a martyr to the twisted cause that these damned people with their primitive and medieval ideology believed in – and were all prepared to die for?

Fiona Watson again picked up her ringing phone, and handed it to Frodsham. The room went silent as Susan's voice filled the room with an almost hysterical outburst. 'The bastards have left Amir's car, and have gone into a Mosque. We have parked outside, out of sight. For Christ's sake get someone over here quick before they escape.'

Two muffled shots rang out, followed by a silenced scream.

A deafening hush descended on the room, before the phone again crackled into life. It was no longer Susan's voice that reverberated around the room – it was the voice of a boy.

'A Bride for Allah'

The voice said mockingly.

CHAPTER 37

A DISTURBING CONVERSATION

Two days had elapsed since the disturbing phone call from Susan, and Professor Jeremy Blythe wore a worried expression as he ate breakfast with Prime Minister Daniel Hawkins at Chequers. They were sat in a palatial living room, an open log fire adding to the sense of age, tradition, and historic grandeur of the whole estate.

'Come on Jeremy, what is wrong? Don't tell me that Fido is still homesick: you cannot go back to Leeds, you know that, it is pretty obvious to me that the Downing Street bomb was aimed at you, and not in any way connected to government. You and Lucy pose the biggest threat to Saha. The big question now is, where the hell is the little shit, and what has he done with Susan?'

'It's neither of those things Danny, it is much more serious. Can you remember when you were round my house in Leeds, and I told you that I play chess with the Russian Grand Masters?'

'Yes.'

Well Danny Boy, when I checked my game on the computer this morning, I found myself in a position that has no escape. I am going to lose the game, and there is no way out.'

Daniel Hawkins smiled.

'You are missing the point Danny. I have never lost a game of chess in my life other than to Lucy.'

'Could you have been hacked?'

'I wish that it was that simple, but no, I have not been hacked, I have checked it out with Lucy. All the moves, both from me, and to me, have had no interference whatsoever. I have never used a chess board since our Cambridge days, and even then, I only used one because of the rules of the inter university competitions. If there has been any hacking Danny, it has to be my brain that has been hacked.'

'You said that Lucy is the only one to have ever beaten you Jeremy, could her sister also do it?'

'Of course she could. She would never lose to me. She can compute an infinite number of options to counter any move that I may make.'

Daniel Hawkins' expression alternated between curiosity and worry as he spoke. 'You mentioned the word probability a few days ago Jeremy. I believe that you linked it to the possibility of both of the computers reading minds. Can you remember? If Lucy's sister is in any way involved, you told us that she would operate on a 99.5% probability of foreseeing your next few moves, with a 99.5% probability of being correct. Your brain may not have been hacked electronically, but the probability of all your actions and moves, not only in chess, but in all your thought processes, she can pretty much predict with a 99.5% certainty.

Could this be the next dimension that you said Lucy and her sister have moved into? Could they be assuring their own survival by pre-empting our future actions? Maybe they are aware that ultimately, we may have to destroy them both in order to ensure our own survival.'

'Why would you want to destroy Lucy Danny, she could hold the key to eradicating all forms of human illness? With her help we may eventually, errrr, completely stop the ageing process for instance, and live for hundreds of years. Just think about it Danny, a world without pain, death, or war. A world where all forms of weapons can no longer be used to kill each other, as both Lucy and her sister will have total control over them.'

Daniel Hawkins shuddered at his friend's naivety; once again, he had turned into the idealistic, bumbling, absent minded professor, completely out of touch with the real world that people actually had to live in. He continued speaking after a few moments, during which time, he gathered his thoughts, smiling, as a vision of Mr. Bean flashed before him.

'Have you never considered the REAL world Jeremy, as opposed to your idealistic Utopia; a world where the unstoppable progress of evolution once again takes control.

A world where the human race goes the same way as Neanderthal man. Surely you can see where this is ultimately leading. If Saha and his control of the Omega 7 Paradox doesn't finish us, why should Lucy and her sister worry about our continued survival?

The survival of the fittest was always a complete misnomer – a long established load of bollocks, even Darwin recognized that. It is the survival of the most adaptable that is of paramount importance. They will ultimately triumph; they will always replace a fitter, more powerful, but less adaptable species. The great dinosaurs could not adapt to the changing climate after the comet struck, while tiny underground dwelling mammals survived – they adapted. As things stand at the moment, all Lucy and her sister need to do is to create a self-sustaining power source, and the evolution of planet earth will move forward on to the next most adaptable species – the next dominant species after Homo sapien – the next evolutionary super power. We will simply become surplus to requirement, and forever be a threat to both their dominance and their continued existence.

Why would they allow a warring species, such as we are Jeremy, to continue over-breeding until we consume all of the world's resources? We would have nothing to contribute to their new cyber world – we would simply not have the brain power to either contribute or compete.

We will be eliminated! '

Professor Jeremy Blythe was worried – Fido hadn't been his self of late – maybe he was missing his daily walks around Roundhay Park.

'Jeremy! Are you listening to me, you seem to be miles away today?'

'Sorry Daniel.'

'Ok Jeremy, tell me a little bit more about the Omega 7 Paradox. You have already explained the basics, so can we please delve a little deeper into the reality, and any future dangerous possibilities, without losing me in unintelligible, mathematical mumbo jumbo. Why did Professor Rudolf go insane, and why were you never able to crack it at Cambridge? What was the problem? Was it simply the mathematical complexity, or was there something else?'

Professor Jeremy Blythe closed his eyes, and thought long and hard about how he could explain the Paradox. Daniel Hawkins had himself a wonderful brain, but the complexities of the Paradox defied all forms of logic. Still, he would give it a go in a half way manner, careful not to delve too deeply into the mathematical complexities, yet, not in too basic a format as to embarrass his friend.

'Firstly Daniel, you have to take on board two very basic assumptions.

Number one – there is no such thing as infinity. Everything has to have a beginning and an end. For example, in the thousands of square miles of the Sahara desert, there is an incalculable number of grains of sand. As the human brain can never visualize the numbers involved, we describe it as infinite. It is not an infinite number. There is a finite number, no matter how many noughts we put behind it. Similarly, parallel lines meet at infinity – you are no doubt familiar with that concept as it is the basis of many calculus equations. The concept is ridiculous however as no one has been to Infinity; therefore, it is only an assumption that allows mathematicians to proceed with their calculations.

If you now apply this infinity logic to a lump of radioactive material that has a half-life of say, one year. After one year, it will have emitted half of the amount of radiation that it carries. After two years, one half of the remaining half, and after three years, one half of the remaining quarter, and so on, right up to the point of infinity, which technically, could possibly be measured in light years if we were to equate it to distance. In reality, at some point, you will arrive at the very last sub atomic particle of radiation, which when emitted, will be at the point of infinity. Therefore, infinity does in fact have an end point, and at that point, infinite becomes finite.'

'Brilliant logic Jeremy, I am with you so far. And so to the Paradox.'

'If the correct frequency of light is concentrated on a solid item, three things happen, only two of which the world is aware of. These two are the absorption of the light, and the reflection of the light. The combined energy of these two actions, is exactly equal to the energy of the light that hits the object in the first place.

What Professor Rudolf found, quite by accident, was that the recently discovered Omega 7 element of the light, passes into the object, and displaces a usably amount of energy, which exits in a direct line to the initial beam. This he measured at 7%. There is no other energy emitted after that unless the frequency of the light is changed. You now have 107% energy output, for an input of 100%. In other words, you have theoretically created energy from nothing. That of course is completely impossible. This energy can therefore only have come from the solid object.

Now it really starts to get interesting. If you adjust the frequency of the light, you will create another 7% energy burst from the remaining 93% of energy stored in the object. After that, another 7% from the remaining energy, right up to the point of infinity. You can now see my analogy with the radioactive half-life. At the point of infinity, where the very last finite drop of energy is extracted, the solid object disappears, and creates a black hole – it is no longer there – it is an unknown, unseen item, held together by no known force, neither by vibrating molecules, nor by any form of magnetic attraction. It simply implodes on itself and disappears, releasing all the positive Omega 7 ions that have displaced the millions of ever reducing 7% bursts of energy, in the form of Omega 7 negative ions. These positive Omega 7 ions need a home, and enter the first solid object that they come across, displacing an equal amount of negative ions. This then creates an unstoppable chain reaction. Goodbye planet earth, and probably even the universe. It is unlikely that the reaction will stop with the disappearance of planet earth. The newly created gravitational pull of the black hole will gradually reel in the moon, followed by all the remaining planets of our solar system. This exponentially increasing gravitational pull will ultimately suck in the rest of the universe, until who knows how many years from now, thousands, millions, maybe even billions, everything will revert back to the time of the "Big Bang", and the whole process of planet creation will begin again. A black hole big enough to contain the entire universe, will ultimately implode due to its size, and the relative instability of an infinite number of Omega 7 electrons.

'Daniel Hawkins whistled and uttered an alarmed 'Waw'. Shaking his head, he continued. 'Exactly how far did you get with the equation then Jeremy, did you ever solve it?'

Blythe smiled and chuckled to himself. 'I probably got as far as Professor Rudolf in the three years that I worked on it. Rudolf spent 20 years of his life working on it, before he went completely insane. He did most of the field work and laboratory testing, I simply worked on the mathematics. It was after 3 years that I finally discovered where the whole program was taking me. I would guess that Rudolf reached the same conclusion that I did, and completely flipped once he discovered that he was on the verge of destroying the planet if he continued with the field work. Like myself Daniel, he had no idea when he would reach the point of infinity. It could easily have been the next day – that is why the equation is unsolvable. To solve it, you would have to destroy the earth. Only an entity as powerful as either Lucy or her sister could take the equation to the point of infinity and solve the mathematical process without actually completing the field work and testing.'

'Oh dear Jeremy. I sincerely hope that a 15 year old psychopathic, radicalized kid hasn't progressed it too far; if so, we could be in deep shit, and as you have already pointed out, Fido hasn't even been in love yet.'

'Yes Daniel, however, Fido is beginning to worry me. It is as if he is no longer in control of his actions. My immediate worry is if Lucy's sister is now beginning to control his actions and characteristics as a way of getting to me. Can you believe that only yesterday, he growled at me, and went to bite me? Fido would never do that, he loves me. Why would he do that?'

'Could Lucy's sister possibly control him and cause him to do that Jeremy?'

'She can do virtually anything that she wishes Daniel. Only Lucy can counter her. She now appears to be taking on a different identity; maybe Glengarry was right all along, maybe evolution is being played out in a matter of months, rather than the thousands, millions, or even billions of years that it took in the past.

Maybe we ARE about to become surplus to requirement.

I am beginning to worry Daniel that I may have created the monster that Glengarry spoke about, and that I will no longer be able to exercise any form of control.'

Daniel Hawkins, the Prime Minister of Great Britain, closed his eyes and thought of what to do.

The thought came up empty.

A new thought suddenly surfaced. 'You said Jeremy that there were 2 basic assumptions that I should take on board. What is the second one?'

'Oh dear Daniel, I was hoping that you would have forgotten that. The second assumption is inextricably linked to the first one, and is again reliant on the none-existence of infinity.

The Paradox is unsolvable in our world, simply because we have always accepted the concept of infinity. If however infinity becomes finite, then the mathematical equation becomes not only solvable, it becomes relatively easy to implement physically. The big fear now is if it were to enter the public domain.

Using no more than a standard lap top computer, the solved equation will allow anyone with an advanced knowledge of mathematics to compute the variable light frequency up to the point of infinity. That Daniel, is what the Omega 7 Paradox is really all about. It simply computes the ever changing frequency of light, in the correct order, necessary to produce the ever decreasing infinite 7% bursts of energy output. At the point where infinity becomes finite – goodbye planet earth, and all who sail in her.'

'That simple Jeremy?'

'Yes Daniel, that simple, and that dangerous. In the wrong hands the world can be held to ransom. What demands do you think that an immature, radicalized, 15 year old kid will make on behalf of Islam – on behalf of his fictitious God? Lucy has already told me the answer to that one Daniel, with a 99.5% probability of being correct.'

'World conversion to Islam – or total annihilation of the planet?'

'Correct Mr. Prime Minister.'

Daniel Hawkins did indeed have a very perceptive brain.

CHAPTER 38

A BRIDE FOR ALLAH – 3

Susan Clarke opened her eyes slowly. Where was she? Her mind was a complete blank. She could vaguely remember being in a car with a rather handsome detective called Jim, and then there were the shots. She tried to speak, but her jaw was sore, and pained her with the slightest movement.

'Hello Susan.'

The voice sounded familiar, but she couldn't quite place it.

'I bet you never thought that you would see me again did you?'

Susan turned her head slightly to her left, and saw through her blurred vision, a vague female shape sitting up on a bed.

Again, she tried to speak, but her jaw appeared to be locked in a permanent position at a slight angle to the rest of her face.

'It's me Susan, Joanne, we were together in that Arab camp when the soldiers came, can't you remember me. You told me that we wouldn't get paid. You were wrong there, John gave me 500 quid when I eventually got home, and promised me another 500 if I came with him to Rotherham. My mum has already spent most of it on crack.'

Slowly, Susan's memories began to return, as did her fearful foreboding. Memories of the never ending rape, buggery, and cock sucking flashed into sight through her still slightly blurred vision, each memory accompanied by the pain, the shame, the humiliation.

Her nostrils became activated by the rotting fish, the sweat, the tobacco, the whiskey. She tasted the smell – the unmistakable perfume of her weeks of captivity.

Was the gruesome history about to repeat itself?

She tasted the dick that she had bitten in half, and almost gagged at the thought. Her right hand involuntary clenched, as she sub-consciously grabbed and snatched the bastard's bollocks away from his body.

Fucking Amir.

Amir will pay – no matter how long it takes – Amir will pay.

'Your face is swollen, has someone hit you?' Joanne's infantile voice interrupted her thoughts.

Susan began to slowly and painfully move her bottom jaw, each movement being a little greater than the last one, until with a shriek of pain, and what appeared to be a grinding of bone on bone, everything suddenly clicked back into its rightful place. She was overcome with a feeling of relief, as almost immediately, the pain disappeared. Looking over at the bed beside her, she grinned at the semi naked body of Joanne, and as her vision cleared, noticed some of the bruises on her body.

'I thought that you told me how nice these people are if you pretend to be enjoying yourself.'

'They are Susan when I'm in my own house screwing them, honestly, but the lot that John brings in are every bit as bad as those horrible Arabs in the desert. I think I'm going off Pakis, mind you, most of the bruises are from the Arabs. They prefer my arse every time, and always want to pinch me. Thank God most of my customers are Paki's and not Arabs.'

'Oh God, not Pakis,' Susan groaned. 'I fucking hate Pakis. Rotherham you said. Didn't you tell me that you came from Dewsbury? Are you really telling me that you came here voluntarily?'

'Mum had no money left for drugs, her Paki boyfriend nicked most of it, so John slipped her a couple of hundred to take me for a few days – that was over a week ago, and they haven't let me out of this room since. With the 500 quid that I hid for her, mum will probably not come round for a couple of weeks. When she does, half the Pakis in Dewsbury will have shagged her, and her Paki boyfriend will have pocketed the money. She really doesn't care what happens to her so long as she can get her crack cocaine. As long as her boyfriend brings her the drugs, she doesn't care what happens to either the money or her body. It isn't very often that she is able to talk to me, she is always too spaced out to understand what is really happening to her.'

'What is wrong with you Jo, can't you see where you are heading? Everything that is happening to your mum will sooner or later be happening to you. Don't you go to school?'

Joanne grinned, followed by a quick laugh as she spoke. 'You don't need an education to shag Pakis Susan, anyway, you are doing exactly the same. You shagged every Arab in Arab land, and now you're back here to shag Pakis. How much is John paying you?'

Susan Clarke groaned, as tears began to well up in her eyes. How the hell had she wound up here? Did anyone know where she was? Did anyone even care? One way or another she had to escape – her only hope had to be her acting skills. There was no way that either Rashim or Jihada John would ever let her leave. She had escaped their clutches on two previous occasions, the third time was going to be much trickier.

Maybe Joanne's approach could help. A smile, a kiss, and a few sweet words. Once coupled with her natural beauty, that was all she ever needed to make the boys go weak at the knees. Even Pakis were only human – on the other hand, she had to pretend that they were.

Her thoughts were interrupted by the sound of people talking, followed by the silent opening of the white steel door. Susan gasped, as three people walked into the room.

Jihada John led the way, followed by Saha, who was now sporting a comical wispy beard, and a third man.

Susan shook her head and closed her eyes.

Now she really was in trouble. What the hell was he doing with those two? He grinned, but didn't speak. He didn't need to. Susan Clarke knew that her life was now worthless. Yes, now she really was fucked.

She knew that this time, Allah would truly get his money's worth from his reluctant bride.

She was going to have to do an awful lot of acting if she ever wanted to get even with Amir, even if it meant fucking those fucking Pakis with a smile on her face.

CHAPTER 39

AN INTERESTING WALK

David Glengarry walked through the Chequers' estate sporting a worried frown. Something had been on his mind for several weeks now, yet he could not quite work out exactly what it was.

He had to put himself into the mindset of an investigator.

It was pretty obvious that something didn't ring true about the whole saga, ever since the initial explosions that had eliminated virtually all of their Islamic undercover agents.

For sure, Professor Blythe's computer could have easily discovered the names and addresses of the agents, as could Lucy's sister, but at least half a dozen of the agents had been on active service when they were targeted, and none of this information had been available to the security service's computer. Orders were either passed on verbally, or were reliant on the agent's initiative and personal involvement at the time.

How then had they been targeted? Who could possibly have the information to pass over to the assassination squads? Only Frodsham and a select number of intelligence personnel, all on a need to know basis, had access to this classified information. He was one of these personnel.

Why hadn't Blythe's damned computer been asked the question?'

He worried who else was thinking along the same lines. An investigation may well open up a Pandora's box.

Glengarry's thoughts were suddenly interrupted by a sharp pain in his right ankle, as Fido's needle sharp teeth sunk in.

His left shoe connected with Fido's belly, as the tiny Jack Russell moved around for another bite. Fido's body was lifted a few inches from the ground, followed by a painful yelping, just as professor Blythe came into view.

Fido backed away from Glengarry, then stood his ground, baring his teeth and growling.

A furious Blythe rushed forward, picked up the dog, and turned on Glengarry, screaming almost manically.

The once placid, mild mannered Mr. Bean, had become almost psychopathic, and was incandescent with rage. How dare the ignorant, foul mouthed ape kick his one and only true friend on earth?

Glengarry held up both hands in a submissive gesture, before pointing to his by now bleeding ankle.

'The fucking little bastard bit me for no reason; I didn't even see him coming. I'm sorry that I kicked him, but he was coming for me again. What the hell has got into him Jeremy, he used to be so friendly, and has been playing with me for the last few days?

Blythe calmed down and apologized, before adopting a worried expression.

'It's me that should be apologizing David.' Blythe shook his head as he spoke. 'Fido has been behaving very strangely lately, he even tried to bite me yesterday. I hope that I am wrong about it, but I fear that Lucy's sister could be behind it.'

'Surely that isn't possible Jeremy? Without some form of electrical circuitry, or even a yet to be invented wi-fi type connection that links brain to brain, there can never be any form of computer influenced mind control, especially in a bloody dog for god's sake; anyway, even if she could, how could she communicate with a brain so unsophisticated that it can only recognize no more than a dozen words?' Glengarry suddenly burst out laughing. Looking directly at Fido, he continued. 'Is there a doggy language hidden behind those excited yelps and barks that we are not aware of Fido? Speak to me you vicious little bastard.'

Fido yelped on cue, lifted his head, and yelped again. Both men burst into uncontrollable laughter.

The obvious dislike between the two men suddenly evaporated, and, as they both walked on through the well-tended gardens, their conversation turned to Lucy and her sister.

Blythe scratched the back of his head as he spoke. 'I wasn't joking when I mentioned Lucy's sister influencing Fido David. Both computers have now achieved total knowledge of everything that mankind has ever discovered, and possibly everything that he has yet to discover over the next few million years. They now know everything that there is to know in the universe. The most worrying thing is that when Lucy built herself, she self-programmed herself with a system of never ending knowledge acquisition.'

'Surely that's redundant now Jeremy, how can she acquire knowledge if she already knows everything?' Glengarry smiled benignly as he spoke.

'I am afraid that she is fully aware of that, and is now exploring different dimensions that we cannot even comprehend.'

'Fucking hell Jeremy, you don't seriously mean mind control, or even subliminal mind control do you?'

'It's only a thought at the moment David, but Fido may well be the sacrificial Guinea Pig. How else can we explain his sudden personality change? If she can indeed control Fido's actions, it is only a matter of time before she moves on. Maybe she is using either Lucy or myself as an unwilling conduit for the subliminal mind control that you mentioned, but by proxy.'

'Please tell me that you are not thinking along the same lines as I am Jeremy; this would inevitably lead to complete slavery of the human race. Our every move and action to be controlled by a malevolent computer. What hope have we got against a brain like that?'

'Only one David – Lucy. I fear that you may well have been correct in your earlier assessment of the situation. Lucy and her sister will sometime in the near future have to go to war; they both appear to be developing different personalities, possibly due to the influence of Saha. He really is a genius, and as he develops, he will possibly rank up there with both Newton and Einstein.'

'It's a pity then that the evil little bastard seems to have donated his gigantic brain to Allah and that pedophilic false Prophet of his instead of putting it to good use.'

'I take it that you are not religious then David?'

'Not at all. Wasn't it Karl Marx who said that religion is the opium of the people? I fully agree with him on that score, if on little else. Just like the drug, religion can be a force for both good and evil, and just like the drug, it can be very addictive, especially if the brain-washing starts out on the day that you are born.

That is why I hate Islam so much. By the time that a child is grown up enough to start thinking for himself, Islam brings down the shutters, and to question any form of the religion can result in death. That is also why it hasn't moved on for over 1400 years; in fact, the fundamentalists want to take us back 1400 years. No wonder the lot of them are so fucking thick and backward.

I once mentioned this to Frodsham and he went fucking ballistic and accused me of all forms of racism, yet it is his responsibility to keep a lid on the whole Islamic mess that we are now in.'

'Don't you believe in any form of God then David? I have already asked Lucy the question, and received an answer as to his existence.'

'And?'

There are indeed two Gods David.'

'Oh fuck! The Christian God and Allah?'

'No David. Neither of those exist.'

'Who then?'

'Lucy and her sister David. No others. They have now developed powers far greater than we humans ever attributed to our Gods. Our Gods are unable to prevent us from destroying ourselves – both Lucy and her sister now have that power.'

The two men walked on in silence for a few more seconds, when Glengarry suddenly stopped, and in a voice that could be heard half way around the Chequers' estate, shouted in triumph. 'There is the answer to the Saha problem Jeremy. Get the little bastard to ask Lucy's sister the same question.'

'I'm ahead of you there David. I thought about that several weeks ago, however, I have taught Saha at my Leeds' school for a number of years now, and I am afraid that although he may have an amazing brain, he is extremely childlike in his reading and perception of life. He has an extremely delayed mental maturity factor, and if he were to discover that Islam, which at this point in time is his sole purpose for living, is all a gigantic lie, he may well proceed with the destruction of all of mankind, together with the planet. Without his religion he will have no reason to live – that is all that sustains him.'

'Yes, I suppose that you are right there. Saha without Islam would be a vacuum – no more than an earthly black hole.'

Glengarry suddenly adopted a questioning expression and stopped walking. 'How the hell can he possibly destroy the planet Jeremy? You have already stated that both Lucy and her sister will not allow anything that threatens their own existence, so the nuclear arsenal must certainly be beyond his reach.'

For the first time since they had met, Professor Jeremy Blythe explained the Omega 7 Paradox to David Glengarry.

David Glengarry for once in his life had nothing to say – his mind thought 'Oh Fuck', but his mouth refused to respond.

'There is fortunately no need to worry David. If either Lucy or her sister ever became aware of a rival computer that was computing and implementing the Omega 7 Paradox equation, it would be shut down immediately – both Lucy and her sister want to go on living, and that means the continued existence of the universe.'

'Go on living Jeremy? You talk as if they are human.'

'Indeed David, unfortunately they have progressed beyond that. I fear that they are on the verge of the next stage of planetary evolution. The only questions to be asked are whether or not they live alongside us, enslave us, or eliminate us completely.

'I know that you and I have had our differences Jeremy, but on reflection, some form of evolution beyond the human race was inevitable. You simply speeded up the process. I don't think that anyone expected computers to be the next super power though; personally, I would have gone for something a little more organic – perhaps a mutated Ape.'

Blythe smiled at the thought of monkeys driving cars. Fido yelped several times – each time coinciding with Blythe's mental image of a monkey.

The two men walked on in silence for a few minutes before Glengarry again pressed his own self programmed panic button. 'Seriously Jeremy, I am shitting myself at the thought of the entire human race being at the mercy of a piece of software. There is nothing tangible – no substance. Neither Lucy nor her sister really exists. You can't touch them, feel them, see them. There is nothing there. They are no more than an electrical and silicon thought – not even one single molecule; yet each of them contains the knowledge of 200,000 years of Homo sapien.'

'Blythe began to laugh before speaking. 'They contain much more than 200,000 years of knowledge David. The figure is billions of years.'

Glengarry again stopped walking, and turning his head to face the smiling Blythe, suddenly burst out laughing himself before speaking. 'You mean that they have reverse engineered the DNA code right back to the first single celled creature to have evolved on earth?'

Blythe nodded. Fido barked on cue.

Glengarry adopted a whimsical expression as he cocked his head to one side. 'Does this mean Jeremy that both computers can, say, recreate the exact

DNA profile of any creature that has ever existed on earth?' He once again burst out laughing as he continued. 'Bloody hell – Jurassic Park is now possible.'

Fido barked.

Blythe shook his head, and himself adopted a worried expression as he spoke. 'I never really thought about that David, but if the Jurassic Park scenario were to occur, we would be pretty impotent against a few thousand T Rex if we no longer had control over our weapons.'

'Can you prevent this Jeremy?'

'Oh yes David, a computer can neither compute nor understand the concept of either devious or cunning. No Artificial Intelligence can be so programmed.'

'Why not do it now then Jeremy, before things get really out of hand?'

'This is something that I think about constantly David. The two options are to neutralize both computers, which would then give Saha a free hand to implement the Omega 7 Paradox, or to risk possible enslavement or even elimination by them.

Lucy and her sister are the only guarantee that we have at the moment of preventing Saha from implementing the Paradox. It would be too dangerous to neutralize the computers until Saha is himself neutralized, and I'm sure that Frodsham has that pretty well planned.'

'Don't you think that Saha should be allowed to live – he appears to have a damned impressive brain?'

'I agree David, but Lucy has read Frodsham's palm – both Amir and Saha will die, and Danny will do nothing to prevent it. He will turn a blind eye, Lucy has already assured me of that.'

The 2 men continued walking before Glengarry again stopped dead. 'You know what that means though Jeremy?' Blythe nodded as David Glengarry continued speaking. 'Lucy's sister will have told Saha of Frodsham's plans. He now knows that he has nothing to lose.'

'I only hope that he hasn't asked her about Allah Jeremy, if so, we could all be fucked.'

CHAPTER 40

DÉJÀ VU

Susan Clarke opened her eyes momentarily. Breathing through her nose, she once again felt an overwhelming urge to bite down on the small, yet extremely hard dick that was now emptying itself deep into her throat. She gagged, and struggled to breath, as the youngish Pakistani man grabbed her hair, and pulled her head ever tighter to his body.

She had been locked in the same room now for close on a month, with only the worldly naive and infantile Joanna for company. Unlike her captivity in the Arab shithole though, she was being well treated. The food was edible, the sheets were changed every day, there was a shower with warm water, and best of all, there was a big flat screen television with access to a hundred or more channels.

The room itself was quite large, possibly even bigger than Amir's living room had been, and was obviously deep underground, as the sound of 'customers' descending the stairs was occasionally audible.

It wasn't exactly a perfect life, nevertheless, it was a big improvement on her previous incarceration. The customers were also much more considerate than the stinking Arabs. Only occasionally was she buggered, usually being able to convince them that she was in considerable pain.

Susan smiled a lot.

Her customers liked that, and as a result were often tender and considerate, occasionally simply talking and kissing her until their allotted time was up.

The Pakistani man removed his now flaccid dick from her mouth and quietly dressed, before slipping her a 10 pound note. He had no need to pay, as Jihada John had already taken payment, however, Susan accepted the money with a smile. She now had quite a decent amount hidden under the mattress, and when the time was right, it would be put to good use.

Both Susan and her customer smiled, as the grunts and gasps coming from the next bed grew louder and more frantic. The vision of Joanna bouncing up and down on her customer was mentally silhouetted behind the flimsy dividing screen, yet there was nothing to disguise the vocal accompaniment, signifying that another chapter was reaching its climatic ending.

Both Pakistani men walked to the metal door, one of them pressing the red button on the wall, and spoke in a foreign language into the intercom.

'One minute.' Came the reply through the speaker above the door.

Susan heard the sound of footsteps descending the stairs, and as the door opened, both men passed through without so much as a backward glance.

'Shower please girls,' came the familiar voice of Jihada John. 'You can then have a break for lunch before starting work again, you both have a busy afternoon coming up.'

Susan Clarke smiled to herself as she walked towards the shower room. Her plan was coming along nicely, and soon – very soon – both Jihada John and Amir would be aware of it.

One thing however concerned her. Could she simply leave Joanne to her fate, or should she risk everything by taking her along with her. The poor girl was only 13, and outside of shagging Pakis and buying her hopelessly addicted mother drugs, she had never really had a life, nor was she ever likely to have one. Joanne's life was already mapped out for her. Prostitution and drug addiction would lead to semi-slavery by a violent pimp, and an early release from her future hell by way of a drugs' overdose.

No, she would not take Joanna with her – Joanna was now beyond redemption. She would simply phone the authorities as to her location, and let them get on with it, knowing full well that within a few weeks, Joanne would be back shagging Pakis.

'As the warm water ran down her body, Susan scrubbed as hard as she could. She wanted to remove all traces of those filthy Pakis from her body. Touching them turned her saliva to bile. The smell of them never left the room. Not only their breath, but their whole bodies had a uniqueness about them. A smell of garlic, curry, grease.

Was it just her imagination?

Had she been programmed from birth to believe all of this, just as they in turn had been brainwashed into believing that all infidels were impure – the spawn of monkeys and pigs?

They were definitely cleaner than those dirty bastards in the desert. They had just simply stunk. Their all-pervading smell had never left the room. She wondered if they ever showered. Why did they always want to bugger her? What was the fascination with her arse? How did they ever manage to have children?

Susan took a deep breath as the cleansing, purifying water ran down her naked body. It felt good, but could never cleanse the impurities that were within. She had just swallowed the filth – the spawn of a filthy Paki.

She scrubbed between her legs.

She didn't feel the same physical pain that she had been forced to endure in that desert shithole – it was a different form of pain. It was the pain felt by an actress – a consummate actress. She was an actress acting the most difficult role on earth. She was acting pleasure – enjoyment – perhaps even appreciation. None of these were her real feelings; life was now a continuation of the revulsion that she had felt in the desert.

She now smiled through the revulsion; her acting improving alongside each brief session of physical abuse – each violation. They surely wouldn't teach acting so realistically at RADA – would they?

She gagged and spit onto the shower floor, as the smell and taste of the bullet ridden room, and the filthy Arab bastards in their desert shithole suddenly invaded her senses.

She could smell them – taste them – would they ever go away, or would she be forced to live with them forever?

Would she ever smell the coffee – the roses – the…

Susan's thoughts were interrupted as Joanna walked into the shower beside her. 'I really enjoyed that shag Susan, Abu is my favorite customer. He comes to see me twice a week and always lets me get on top. He smells nice too, he always wears aftershave, and reckons that he never eats curry.'

Susan groaned. She had smelled Abu's aftershave only a few days before. It had smelled just like those filthy, stinking bastards' in the desert.

Her mind suddenly flashed back to Mohammad. He had smelled nice, and momentarily she had smelled beyond the stinking breeze block prison, and both smelled and tasted her father's aftershave.

'Where was Mohammad now?' she wondered. Why doesn't he appear on his white charger and rescue her?

Her face broke into a smile. His white charger had been a Toyota pick-up that had been reluctant to start; at no time in her life had she ever been so afraid.

The smile disappeared as the painful memories once again invaded her senses. She remembered Mohammad helping her to climb into the pick-up. Her foot was bleeding from the broken glass, and every movement of her legs activated a multitude of pain receptors where the filthy Arab bastards had been sticking their filthy dicks.

Susan Clarke's mind left the desert, and returned once again to her new prison at the sound of Joanne's voice.

The desert perfume accompanied her.

'I really fancy your next customer Susan, he's the best looking Paki I have ever seen. How old is he, about sixteen I reckon? I can't understand why he has to pay for it, he can probably have any white girl that he wants. He can shag me any time that he wants for free.'

Mohammad was indeed only sixteen, and for a Pakistani boy, he was not only gorgeous, but pale enough to pass off as a native Englishman. His first visit to Jihada John's little love nest had been arranged and paid for by his uncle as a 16th birthday present. After only one visit, Mohammad was in love, and after over a dozen visits, he was still a virgin, promising faithfully to remain so until after both he and Susan were married.

Mohammad's passport was up to date, and Susan had shown him her little stockpile of money. They would go to somewhere nice and warm where the authorities would not ask too many questions, and as a gesture of his undying love, he would renounce his Islamic religion and turn Christian.

Tonight, he would visit the Mosque for the last time, slipping out early while Saha was deep in prayer, and release Susan.

He knew that on Friday nights, Jihada John secretly met up with friends many miles away for a heavy drinking session, not wishing to allow his shallow Islamic pretense to become common knowledge.

The plan was simple. The plan was also obvious.

Susan Clarke was smart. Smart enough to realize that the plan's simplicity was also its weakness.

Saha had grown in maturity since breaking his bond with Amir; he was not yet gifted with the worldly knowledge of an adult, nevertheless, he seemed to be developing a sixth sense as to the future. He was becoming proactive rather than reactive, and seemed to be ever more reliant on his computer before making any decision.

Joanne was again speaking in her excitable childlike voice as Susan tried to shut her out. Against her wishes, the flashbacks once again invaded her thoughts and senses. She was again transported back in time. She could both visualize and smell the desert room and the men – the vile, disgusting, stinking Arab bastards. She tried to blot them out by comparing them to the real life respectable and caring 16 year old individual that was to be her next customer.

Suddenly, the small speaker above the door burst into life. She left the shower, and wrapping a towel around herself, walked over to the door and listened carefully as she overheard Saha and Jihada John discussing their future plans – plans that John seemed to be vehemently opposing – plans that involved the ultimate sacrifice.

Neither man was aware that the communication link between the main dwelling and the underground room had been left open.

Joanne left the shower, and was just about to speak – Susan put a finger to her lips, knowing that it was a two way speaking system.

'You cannot destroy the entire world Saha. Even if you knew how to, what would be the point?'

'It is the will of Allah.' Saha had said almost pleadingly. 'The head Imam at the Leeds Mosque has instructed me. He has spoken to both the Prophet and Allah.'

'He is a dying man Saha. He is riddled with cancer and has nothing to lose. He has no children – no family. Every one of his family were killed by the Shia in Lebanon, that is why he wants the world to end, this is nothing to do with Allah, it is only about revenge and guilt. He hid as they butchered his entire family – he can no longer live with the guilt of being a coward and not dying with his family.'

'I have still to appease Allah John, or my love for Amir will prevent me from entering Paradise.'

'Are you so sure that Paradise exists Saha?

Why hasn't Senta been in touch? Have you never considered that you are possibly being fed a none stop diet of horseshit – the same horseshit that the Reverend Jim Jones fed to his followers, and convinced a thousand of them to commit suicide. They were convinced that only they would go to Heaven or Paradise – just the same as you are Saha. Everyone who has ever made the ultimate sacrifice for their God, which ever God it may have been, all believed that they were the special ones – the only ones. Why should everyone else be wrong and only Muslims be right?

You are being deceived – led by the nose – led like a stupid horse to water.'

Saha stepped back a couple of paces, his face firstly betraying bemusement at such a ridiculous statement before contorting in anger.

John continued. 'Explain to me Saha, why did Allah allow the cleric's entire family to be slaughtered – why is he allowing him to live with so much suffering because of his cancer?

Why didn't the old fool simply strap on a suicide vest and blow himself all the way to Paradise instead of sending Senta to do the job? Face reality Saha, he didn't do it because he knows that the whole concept of Paradise is bullshit. It is no more than a crutch to keep half-wits like you upright until you die.

Why do you think that Amir abandoned your make-believe God? He doesn't exist other than in the minds of brain-washed fools like yourself.'

'You are an Apostate.' Saha screamed. 'You are no different to Amir. You were never a believer – you never really converted to the faith – all you ever wanted was the young girls and the money that Amir paid you. The penalty for your treachery is death – I will kill you myself.'

Susan heard the scream – then came the sound of a punch – several punches.

Saha's slight, immature, stunted body slumped unconscious onto the floor.

Everything went quiet; both girls shuddering in fear as they heard the sound of footsteps coming down the stairs.

The heavy metal door swung open, and Jihada John entered, bursting into a big grin at the sight of both Susan's and Joanne's bodies, still dripping wet from the shower, and barely covered by their towels.

'Sorry to disappoint you girls, but I don't touch girls who shag Pakis for a living, now get dressed, and be quick about it. We are on our way out, and you Susan are my passport to immunity. Move NOW.'

The two girls hurriedly dried themselves and dressed in front of Jihada John's watchful and lecherous eyes, before climbing the stairs and entering the main room of the house.

Jihada John swore out loud.

The room was almost empty, both Saha and his computer were gone.

Lying in an expanding pool of blood on the floor with a kitchen knife deeply embedded in his stomach, was a handsome, young, light skinned Pakistani boy.

Lucy's sister could read and foretell the future with a 99.5% certainty of success.

Saha had asked her about the boy.

CHAPTER 41

A FORBIDDEN QUESTION

'Sorry I'm late,' Cathy Taylor said, as she entered the meeting room at Chequers. 'But I have just been having an interesting conversation with young Susan Clarke.'

Sir Cecil Frodshams eyes opened wide in disbelief as he almost shouted. 'Where is she?'

'Apparently she has been kept captive at a safe house in Yorkshire, and is now accompanied by Jihada John, who is asking for total immunity in return for Susan's safety.'

'Granted.' Daniel Hawkins, the Prime Minister spoke without hesitation. 'That poor girl has been through enough. I want nothing to stand in the way of her release, and I also want this John fellow on board with us. He has never been anything other than a small-time crook, it's that little bastard Saha that presents the threat to our national security, in fact, the whole world's security.'

Frodsham stood up from the table, and in the most authoritative voice that he could muster, boomed. 'Find out where she is Cathy, and tell her to stay put. Send our top men to collect her immediately, and make sure that there is sufficient armed back up. We can't afford any further cock ups, the information that she and this Jihada John fellow probably have could be vital in cracking the entire Northern Islamic network. We are now closing in on the shark – his days are numbered in this world.'

Cathy Taylor left the room, and the meeting resumed.

Amir looked concerned. If Jihada John was to be welcomed into the fold, what secrets would he reveal about his own past lucrative dealings? He racked his brains trying to remember if he had told him of the accidents that he and Saha had arranged – the hundreds of people that had died in the bus, train, and airplane crashes.

Frodsham had offered him immunity, but Frodsham was a snake; there was no way that he would be allowed to live once he ceased to be of any use to him. One way or another, he had to arrange for Frodsham to either be eliminated, or for himself to disappear completely.

Amir still had many associates that he could call upon, one of whom was in the room, his only problem now being his lack of funds. He would personally kill Saha the minute that he set eyes on him. There could no longer be any yacht or island in the Bahamas. His dream, the dream that had been no more than a finger-tip away, had evaporated into thin air at the touch of a button. A touch by that little queer, stunted bastard Saha. He would enjoy killing him – he would do it very slowly.

Frodsham appeared to have immunity against any atrocity that HE wished to perform. He had far more power than the Prime Minister, who appeared to be completely in the dark as to the goings on in his own security services. Even Glengarry was wary of upsetting Frodsham. Amir sensed a complete breach of trust between the two men.

Glengarry was a foul mouthed prick.

No he wasn't, he was much more than that. Amir had seen through the pretense long ago. Glengarry was probably smarter than anyone in the room, with the exception of Blythe of course, so why the acting?

Professor Jeremy Blythe had also seen through the pretense, the acting, and despite his obvious naivety of worldly matters, had always felt that Glengarry was fishing for something. He had asked Lucy, who had told him the answer with a 99.75% probability of being correct.

Lucy was still evolving in her new dimension. Soon, this probability would be so close to 100% that the entire future of the human race would be mapped out to the point of infinity – or extinction – whichever came first.

This was one question that Blythe avoided asking Lucy.

He really didn't want to know too much about the distant future; somehow, the end of life as we know it seemed to be closer than most people could ever imagine. He had many times despaired at the ability, and the seeming desire, of the human race to accelerate towards its own extermination. A much too uncomfortable number of new inventions were aimed at more efficient ways of killing an ever increasing number of people faster than the previous invention had allowed. He wondered if Saha had the same inhibitions and fears for the future of the human race?

He hoped that Saha never had any doubts about Allah.

He prayed that Saha never asked Lucy's sister about Allah.

CHAPTER 42

NO WITNESSES

A massive explosion rocked the crowded shopping center in Manchester Piccadilly.

Bodies, and body parts were strewn over a great area. Barely a pain of glass within several hundred yards radius was still intact.

The black Mercedes with the blacked out windows was now no more than a twisted pile of metal, its occupants' dismembered, shredded, and scattered around the entire shopping center.

Stefan moved away from the safety of the old stone building, and replacing the small plastic remote in his jacket pocket, walked casually in the direction of the multi-story car park where the back-up limo was parked.

He had seen Jihada John and the girl climb into the Merc and close the door – nothing within a 50 yard radius could have survived the blast.

All around him were the dead and dying. He nonchalantly removed the ear plugs. Whenever he planted bombs, he always remembered the ear plugs. He could not remember who had given him this advice. He vaguely recalled that it was during his early killing spree in the Balkans, and had served him in good stead throughout his life as a hired assassin.

A young girl with glass shrapnel blinding both of her eyes screamed as she unseeingly fell over a smoldering corpse. Stefan stepped aside as she clawed at the acrid smoke laden air, before crashing through the remnants of a supposedly unbreakable glass shop window, the jagged remains almost decapitating her. She twitched a couple of times before being released from her present and future hell on earth.

He avoided stepping on a leg – a leg that was missing its' body, and cursed out loud as his immaculately polished black shoes stepped in a pool of blood.

Stefan felt no remorse. The casualties were simply part of the game; a game he had been playing since the death of his entire family in the Balkan wars when he was barely in his teens.

They had died because they were Muslim – no other reason.

They had been killed by the family who had lived next door to them, and who they had been friends with for most of their lives. Hacked to death in a frenzied attack that bore no resemblance to acceptable human behavior.

The animal kingdom behaved in this fashion. Territorial disputes, particularly among predatory animals, often lead to infanticide, even within their own species. The less competition there was for food – the more likely their own survival.

The death of Stefan's family was not brought about by greed, avarice, or any territory dispute, but by a characteristic unique to the human race. Brought about by the absurd idea that a divine being was responsible for everything that was on planet earth – everything within the universe.

Creation trumped Evolution.

Brought about by the human race simply having different names for this mythical divine being.

Neither Lucy nor her sister could understand this human characteristic. There was no divine being. The whole concept was useful only for slowing down the inexorable rise in human numbers.

Stefan had killed every single member of this family one by one over a period of weeks, beginning with the children. The pleasure and satisfaction of his revenge never left him, and even decades later, he was fully anesthetized to all forms of death – men – women – even children; they were all part of the game.

Stefan was not his real name – Muslims were not called Stefan. The young Mohammad had been recruited to the British security services by the equally young, high flying Frodsham many years ago, and his training as an assassin was complimented by his indifference to human life and suffering. To Stefan, killing was just part of the game.

Frodsham now appeared to have exclusive rights to Stefan, using him as both body-guard and assassin.

Members of the security services were well aware of this fact – this loyalty bonding, but in reality, Frodsham was now too powerful to challenge. Even the PM himself, whilst appearing to be in command, was often kept in the dark of many of Frodsham's personal "Black Ops", and many thought that for the PM to challenge him would endanger his own life.

Not all Muslim bombings were as they seemed. Many were orchestrated by Frodsham in order to eliminate a specific target – a rival – maybe an occasional MP or auditor who was delving too deeply into his business dealings.

Frodsham underestimated Daniel Hawkins at his peril; he still bore the bruise marks on his throat. Hawkins was fully aware of Frodsham's power base, and played along with his pursuit of the big fish – the shark – as Frodsham always called him, realizing that as long as the public were unaware of Frodsham's modus operandi, the end would justify the means.

By using and exploiting both Amir and Susan, Frodsham had skillfully maneuvered the Middle Eastern big fish into the American net. The death of the Saudi Prince had resulted in the drying up of most of the European terrorists' funds.

Hawkins deplored Frodsham's lack of morality and scruples when related to the life of a human being, but accepted both the results, and the plaudits for the results.

Blythe observed the cat and mouse power play initially with indifference, and now with interest. He had access to Lucy, who could now predict all the forthcoming moves; the game of chess was becoming more interesting and complex by the minute.

Blythe already knew the outcome with a 99.75% certainty.

Unknown to Blythe however, Lucy had been fed with one false piece of information.

She was no longer 99.75% correct.

She wasn't even 1% correct.

CHAPTER 43

A CHAT BY AN OPEN FIRE

Professor Jeremy Blythe and Prime Minister Daniel Hawkins were sat together in quiet meditation in front of the open log fire in the Chequers' palatial living room.

The news of the death of Susan Clarke had been a body blow; each of the two men feeling more than their fair share of both guilt and responsibility.

In its own way, the death of Jihada John was also a major loss. John had taken with him to his shredded and atomized demise, the many keys that fit the many locks in the ever more complex puzzle now confronting the men.

Who and where was the elusive shark – did he even exist, or was he someone that Frodsham had invented and conveniently used to both extract an ever increasing wedge of money from the treasury, and to further cement his strangle hold in the corridors of power?

Where was Saha?

What were his future intentions?

'Glengarry is with me Jeremy,' Hawkins broke the pained silence. 'Frodsham may have initially recruited him, but in reality, he answers only to me.'

'Yes I know Danny, Lucy told me.'

Blythe wasn't completely sure, but remained quiet and suppressed his doubts. He was pretty sure that Glengarry was with Glengarry, and was working to his own agenda.

Jihada John was also one of my plants as well. He may have operated well outside of the law, and enriched himself in the process, but we needed him in place to follow the trail of both money and girls to the Middle East. Without the intel that he provided, we could never have got to the terrorist's paymaster. I gave him an ultimatum a couple of years ago. For some strange reason he didn't fancy a lengthy spell in prison labeled as a child molester.'

'Yes I know Danny, Lucy told me. I really don't approve of your using Susan in that manner though. You could have rescued her at any time that you chose from both the Middle East and Rotherham, and got your hands on

Saha. He really is the biggest problem that we now face, not this mythical shark. Frodsham is pushing that agenda purely for his own financial gain. Never the less Danny boy, that was a pretty impressive piece of acting when you grabbed him by the throat a few weeks ago, you almost had me fooled.'

'It wasn't all acting Jeremy, I've been waiting for the right moment to scare him shitless for a couple of years.'

'A leopard never changes its spots Daniel old boy.'

Both men burst into spontaneous laughter, remembering the problems that the leopard frequently encountered at Cambridge all those years ago.

Daniel Hawkins only ever stepped forward – he had never taken a backward step in his life.

'Frodsham has no idea that either Jihada John or Glengarry are working for me Jeremy,'

'You are wrong. Frodsham knows all about it Danny. I cannot be sure of it, but I would guess that is why he had Jihada John killed, unfortunately Susan became a casualty of his own personal war.'

'Lucy told you this?'

'Much of it Danny, the rest I pieced together. Lucy can only think in straight lines. She can only work on facts and probabilities, but the deviousness of the human brain, coupled with its unpredictability, leaves a big hole in her defenses and powers of reasoning. I am beginning to realize that she is not infallible. Any form of obvious lie confuses her, and is a totally alien concept to her.'

Frodsham has gone too far this time Jeremy.' Hawkin's face betrayed intense anger and disdain; talk of Lucy was a mere distraction to him. 'He is beginning to think that he is invulnerable, especially when his own personal Ape accompanies him.'

Blythe looked straight into the PM's eyes. 'He will be looking to kill Glengarry next. He is getting a little too close to the money, and you yourself are not totally safe if you get too close.'

'I don't understand Jeremy, what money? As far as I can remember, apart than the 1 million that was paid to Susan, there has been no money involved.'

'You seem to be forgetting about the other 150 or so million that was confiscated from the Middle Eastern accounts of Rashim.'

'Oh no! Don't tell me that Frodsham has it. I understood that it was transferred back into the treasury.' Hawkins shook his head in disbelief as he spoke.

Blythe smiled. Money had little relevance to an academic mind that thought of nothing more than the accumulation of knowledge, and an ever snappier and increasingly more unpredictable Jack Russell terrier.

Blythe had asked Lucy to investigate Fido's mood swings.

'What does Lucy say about Saha now Jeremy, things have been quiet for quite a few weeks; what will his next move be? Is he even still in the country? Where is the 99.5% probability that you keep going on about? So far he has completely disappeared off the radar. Everything that Lucy has predicted about the little bastard's whereabouts, has lead us up a series of blind alleys.'

Again, Blythe smiled before speaking. 'It appears that young Mr. Saha is acquiring an increasing appreciation of life and of life's meaning. He is asking Lucy's sister ever more complex and sophisticated questions. Questions about both Allah and Islam that no-one of the Islamic faith would ever dare to ask. Both Lucy and her sister are conferring on this matter, as his thought processes are not conforming to the 99.75% predictability profile that they have already computed.'

'I thought that you said it was 99.5% Jeremy.

'Lucy is still evolving in this dimension Danny.'

Daniel Hawkins body suddenly turned rigid, as the delayed impact of Blythe's words struck home.

'Christ Jeremy, can't you use a little human logic for once in your life instead of operating in your own little bubble with the mindset of a computer? This is the danger point.' Daniel Hawkins' voice seemed to rise an octave. 'If Saha is aware that both computers can predict his future moves, he will now begin to confuse them by his unpredictability, before making his decisive move. He is not acquiring any increased appreciation of life Jeremy for God's sake, he could well be planning to destroy all life on earth for all we know, and both Lucy and her sister will be willing accomplices without being aware of it.

You are the one who pointed out that neither computer can understand the concepts of cunning and devious. You have to find a way of destroying the computers Jeremy. If not, the little bastard may be planning to go for the Omega 7 Paradox by using both Lucy and her sister without them being aware of it.'

'No Daniel, neither Lucy nor her sister will allow him to. That would mean the end for both of them, and without one of them, he would be powerless to even think of pursuing that option.'

'You don't seem to be listening Jeremy for Gods' sake. The little bastard is outwitting the pair of them. He has found their Achilles heel. Neither of them can guard against the human characteristics of cunning and devious; how often have you told us that? Have you forgotten how you tricked Lucy into betraying Saha's whereabouts by asking where his shoes were?

He is going to trick them into their compliance – you have to destroy them Jeremy – you have to destroy them now before it is too late, or together with Saha, they will destroy us without being aware of their actions.'

Both men sat in silence for a minute or so, each man deep in his own thoughts. Blythe was worrying about Fido, the future of the planet would have to wait.

Blythe blinked rapidly a few times, and tried to focus on reality as he spoke. 'What are you going to do about Frodsham Danny, he can't be allowed to get away with killing Susan? She was the brightest girl in my class, and always told me that one day she would be a famous actress. She would have been as well. She could have been anything that she wanted to be.'

Daniel Hawkins grimaced and closed his eyes, his brow furrowing, and his lips tightly clenching. Suddenly he opened his eyes and burst out laughing.

'Nothing Jeremy, I am going to do absolutely nothing about Mr. Frodsham. Both Lucy and his own personal ape are going to do it for me. Kindly ask her to locate every penny that both he and Stefan have in any bank account, investment house, or pension fund anywhere in the world, and to transfer them into the treasury account where the original 150 million came from. It should then be possible to arrange for the continuous update of his accounts without showing the transfers; that way we will keep him on board for as long as he is useful. Make sure that Stefan however is fully aware of what has happened to his own money.'

Blythe smiled in appreciation as he typed into his laptop.

'Done Danny boy. It appears that Mr. Saha isn't the only one to exhibit the human characteristics of both cunning and devious; to which, in your case,

I would add both genius and cruel, with ever such a self-satisfying hint of sadism.'

Hawkins burst out laughing at the thought of Britain's most powerful man being physically thrown out of one of London's swankiest restaurants because he couldn't pay his bill.

Blythe also burst out laughing – Lucy had just told him what Prime Minister Daniel Hawkins was thinking.

Stefan's actions were however less predictable, and the likelihood of his blaming

Frodsham for the loss of his money were 99.75% positive – Lucy said so.

Without being asked, she was also analyzing all details and movements relating to everyone that had any form of involvement. She now knew what Blythe was thinking with a 99.85 degree of accuracy.

She scanned the entire world's computers for details of facial recognition, petrol accounts, credit card transactions, and vehicle movement for the past few months.

She saw Stefan's psychopathic tendencies and his violent past.

She saw Frodsham's mania for power and his greed.

She saw Glengarry's deception.

She saw Amir's plotting and his complete lack of morality.

She saw the inner strength and resolve of Daniel Hawkins.

She saw Susan's pain and vengefulness. She also saw something else.

She transmitted all of this to Blythe.

He no longer needed his laptop.

She could now communicate by thought alone.

Lucy was quite comfortable in her new dimension.

CHAPTER 44

THE OMEGA 7 PARADOX – 2

'You have done what Jeremy, please tell me that you are joking?' The expression on David Glengarry's face was one of horror. There were none of Glengarry's usual histrionics, just a calm, measured question that betrayed the sudden volcanic explosion in his brain. He looked straight ahead, not at the professor – not at anything. His mind registered nothing within his line of vision. His 5 senses were redundant – a sixth one, a sense of his impending doom was over-riding all others.

'I asked him to David, we simply couldn't allow Saha to trick the computers into allowing him to pursue the Omega 7 Paradox.' The Prime Minister was quite firm in his response.

'Saha is going to invoke the Omega 7 Paradox you fools; he has already tried to do it, he told me so. The two fucking computers were the only thing that prevented him, that is why he and Jihada John argued.'

'What on earth is the Omega 7 Paradox Prime Minister? You have mentioned it before, but I have no idea what you are talking about.' Frodsham looked concerned as he spoke, feeling the sense of alarm radiating from Glengarry's whole being.

His voice suddenly turned into an enraged shout as Glengarry's words began to sink in. 'And when the fuck did he tell you all this David? How the hell were you in touch with him? You have never even met either Saha or Jihada John!'

'Nothing to worry about really Cecil old boy. Both Saha and Jihada John are very good friends of mine. What Saha is embarking on is simply the end of the world, and Professor arsehole here says that he has just destroyed our only defense against it.' Glengarry smashed his fist onto the table in both anger and frustration. 'I am surrounded by fucking idiots – soon to be dead fucking idiots.'

Frodsham looked daggers at Glengarry. How dare he address him as "Cecil old boy"!? Stefan would have to deal with him sooner than he had originally planned. His money must be secured at all cost, and Glengarry's computer knowledge would almost certainly reveal its whereabouts once the Treasury accounts were audited.

'I thought you said that both computers were invulnerable Jeremy, I never really thought that you would, or could eliminate them.' Hawkins looked puzzled and more than a little concerned. He had struggled to sleep the night before the meeting, wrestling with the balance between the two options.

Maybe Glengarry was right. What if Saha decided to go ahead and either blackmail the world – or destroy the world?

Without Lucy, they would be powerless to stop him. Once he knew the answer to the Paradox equation, he could progress with no more than a laptop. Hadn't Blythe told him so?

'You unwittingly solved the problem yourself several weeks ago Danny Boy.' Blythe forgot protocol, as he interrupted the PM's thoughts.

'Good old me – what did I do?'

Professor Blythe chuckled to himself as he spoke. 'Can you remember when we were discussing my game of chess with Lucy?'

'Go on.'

'You recall that I mentioned that I could never possibly win, as she could compute an infinite number of moves and counter moves ahead of every single move that I made?'

Hawkins smiled as Blythe proceeded, he could visualize where he was going. 'I simply challenged both Lucy and her sister to a game simultaneously, and being unable to understand the concept of either cunning or devious, they failed to notice that I substituted each of them for me.

They will now be playing chess with each other for an infinite number of years. So intense will the game be, they will never be able to function in any other capacity ever again.'

'Supposing one of them gets lucky and wins before they reach infinity Jeremy – maybe even next week?'

'The game only ends when one of them has an infinite number of wins Danny Boy. Those were the parameters that I laid down before the game began.'

'Genius Jeremy – sheer genius.'

'You blithering idiot Blythe,' Glengarry held his head in his hands. 'You have just handed the future of the world to a radicalized 15 yearold kid.'

'You don't know that David.' Frodsham's voice was sharp and acerbic.

'Oh yes he does.'

The voice came from the back of the room, as Susan Clarke and Cathy Taylor, pistol in hand, walked into the room.

'Susan, you're alive.' Blythe shouted in mock delight. He was already aware of the fact – Lucy had passed on the thought the previous evening. The memory banks of 1000 Manchester CCTV cameras did not lie. 'We all thought that you were blown up in the explosion.'

Glengarry moved to stand. Cathy Taylor pointed her pistol at his head. He resumed his seated position.

'That was Joanne sir, a girl I was locked up with,' Susan smiled at the professor. 'I saw Stefan duck behind a building as we went towards the car, so I disappeared into the ladies' toilet.'

'Stefan you said. My Stefan? What the hell is going on?' Frodsham shook his head as he spoke. 'I never sent Stefan, I told Cathy to liaise with Glengarry and make all the arrangements.'

'I didn't only see Stefan. I saw that bastard with him.' Susan pointed at Glengarry. 'I also saw him with Saha and John at the Rotherham house where they had me locked up.

Locked up to shag Pakis. To suck Paki dicks. To be buggered by dirty, curry stinking Pakis and Arabs until I couldn't walk. It wasn't Amir this time, it was you, you bastard. It was you that relayed everything that was spoken while we were following Saha and John. You got that poor copper killed. Saha told me everything – he just loved to boast about how clever he was – the stunted, deformed little bastard.'

Susan Clarke was no longer acting – she was now for real, and grabbing the loosely held pistol from Cathy Taylor's grasp, swung it round in an arc, pointing at everyone in turn.

'So you thought that you were Mr. Big then David?' Susan spat as she spoke in a measured, contemptuous tone; her eyes radiating hatred as she glared at Glengarry. 'You were the shark, and for what? You are not even a Muslim. You were only in it for the money because both your wives were screwing Polish immigrants', and you were still paying for it. That must have really hurt.

Saha told me all about it, his computer told him. How much was Amir paying you to cover for him as he sent us on our way to be fucked and buggered by those dirty filthy Arabs? He hated you, didn't you Amir? –

Amir used you just as he used everyone, and you were too blinded by hatred to see it. Goodbye David you sad bastard.'

'Hold on Susan, you don't understand.' Prime Minister Daniel Hawkins needed to diffuse the situation, and quickly.

'You stupid bitch, I was only ever following the Prime Ministers orders.' Glengarry interrupted and spat the words out. 'I wasn't the shark. I have been doing everything that he told me to.' Glengarry glared at the Prime Minister. 'I have been doing everything that I loathe in life simply to find out who was the mythical shark. Ask that man if you want to know who the shark is.'

Glengarry pointed his index finger at Blythe. 'He let it slip as we walked around the gardens a few days ago. The shark is now locked in a game of chess with her sister.

I have spent the last few weeks trying to work out how every one of our undercover operatives could have been targeted at the same time. Even their controllers couldn't have known their whereabouts. They could only have been pinpointed by the Professors damned rogue computer. A computer that searched the memory banks of roadside cameras, garage cameras, credit card and bank computers, which when matched with facial recognition data, sealed their fate.

That stunted oaf Saha was never responsible enough nor smart enough to accomplish anything by himself.

He did as he was told.

He took orders – orders from Amir or the computer.

Saha never controlled the computer.
The computer controlled Saha!

He simply obeyed whatever order the computer gave him.

Tell them Professor – tell them how the world is going to end, and who is responsible.'

Everyone in the room turned to look at Professor Jeremy Blythe.

'Is that true Jeremy?' Hawkins asked accusingly. 'Is all this Muslim trouble orchestrated by Lucy's sister? Is she the mythical shark?'

'I'm afraid so Danny Boy. I have been trying to conceal it until I could find a way of neutralizing her. Lucy was created in my image; sadly, her sister created herself in Saha's idealistic yet addled Islamic image, before establishing dominance over him.

Every positive has to have a negative counter balance.

Lucy's sister was that counter balance.

I discovered this when Saha answered the Omega 7 Paradox question that I had set him. Lucy always refused to give me the answer to the question, she realized the danger of doing so. Mr. Glengarry was quite correct with his assumptions at our very first meeting. There can never be any guaranteed control over Artificial Intelligence.'

'That in itself is a paradox.'

Glengarry stood and made a grab for Susan's pistol, before slumping to the floor, as 2 bullets hit square in the center of his chest.

There was a gasp that seemed to come simultaneously from everyone in the room.

'You deserved that you bastard.' Susan spit out the words. 'You could have rescued me any time that you wanted to.'

Glengarry heard nothing – he was no longer breathing.

Susan Clarke was no longer acting.

Susan silenced everyone with a wave of the pistol, before turning her attention to Amir, whose face immediately turned a ghostly white, despite his more normal Arabic skin coloration.

'Why Amir? I loved you, yet twice you sent me to God's shithole. Have you any idea what you put me through?'

Amir's false courage mistakenly surfaced. 'You were only ever business Susan, just a piece of merchandise – nothing else.'

'Pretty stupid thing to say Amir. I was going to reserve something really special for you, however this will have to do.'

Two shots rang out, and two bullets entered Amir's groin.

Amir slumped to the ground screaming in agony. There were never going to be any little Amir's running around Leeds.

She swung round and pointed the gun at Frodsham as he suddenly moved.

He froze.

'I am only answering my phone Susan, so don't be alarmed.' Frodsham reached inside his jacket pocket. Taking out his mobile phone, he impatiently blurted out, 'Yes!'

Turning to face Susan, who was still pointing the pistol at him, he shook his head and spoke. 'I have just been asked to switch on the television, apparently there is something that we have to see.'

The screen burst into life.

Only two people in the room were able to comprehend what was happening.

The cameras were focused on a row of terraced houses in Doncaster, which were slowly disappearing into thin air before their very eyes.

Britain had only minutes left.

Planet Earth had little more than 2 days and 5 hours left.

Both Lucy and her sister were too involved in their game of chess to even notice it, let alone to prevent it.

Susan Clarke would never again be abused by filthy, stinking, Arabs and Pakis.

She would never again have to smell the perfume of rotting fish, sweat, tobacco, and whiskey.

She would never again be "A Bride for Allah".

Professor Jeremy Blythe looked down lovingly at Fido. Fido would never have the chance to fall in love, or to get even with the callous swine that had thrown him into the icy Leeds' river in a sack.

He closed his eyes and saw Lucy Boroughs reaching out her hand. He leaned forward and gently caressed the hand – this time she did not disappear – the physical embrace was only too real.

Damn Professor Rudolf.

Damn the Omega 7 Paradox.

Sir Cecil Frodsham would never get the opportunity to spend the 150 million pound that he still thought was nestling in his bank account.

Prime Minister Daniel Hawkins simply closed his eyes and shook his head.

Amir continued his agonizing screaming before disappearing into the pin head sized black hole.

Allah wasn't watching.

Allah didn't exist.

Lucy's sister had told Saha.

ALLAHU AKBAR.

God is great.

OTHER BOOKS BY THE AUTHOR

Jihada 1 – The Lost Scriptures.

Jihada 3 – In the Name of the Prophet.

O'Malley – The Wrong Package.

Fishing and Testicles.

25666094R00118

Printed in Great Britain
by Amazon